2.00

All While the Gods Watched

By

Erik Schumann

Copyright © 2004 by Erik Schumann

ISBN 0-7414-1719-7

Published by:

INFIⱭITY
PUBLISHING.COM

519 West Lancaster Avenue
Haverford, PA 19041-1413
Info@buybooksontheweb.com
www.buybooksontheweb.com
Toll-free (877) BUY BOOK
Local Phone (610) 520-2500
Fax (610) 519-0261

Printed in the United States of America

Printed on Recycled Paper

Published November 2003

Dedication

Dedicated to my loving wife, Kim for... well for everything wonderful. And to the Generals when she is not with me.

Table of Contents

Introduction i

Tomorrow and Tomorrow 1

All While the Gods Watched 16

Thanksgiving At Sugar Loaf 20

Lot 1412 40

Lullaby 51

Sharks and Minnows 53

Red Rover 66

Black Stone 79

A Pock of Lips 82

Introduction

This to me is the hardest part of the book to write. Why? Because this is the one section where you actually hear from me, the author, Erik Schumann, pleased to meet you – if I already haven't. And if you have ever heard your own voice on audiotape and cringed, then this is how it is for me right now because everything else in this book you'll read and *hear* with your own voice. That is what I enjoy about writing. I like the anonymity of it all. I've been a ghost writer, a technical writer, a fiction writer (of course) and I think enjoyed being a ghost writer the best because anyone reading the words heard someone else's voice saying them. For example, the President doesn't write his speeches but could or would you want to know the person that put those words in the President's mouth?

Of course you would. I don't know, maybe not. Who really cares?

You will notice there is no picture of me on the jacket of this book. That is completely intentional. Let you guess what I look like, what my voice sounds like, for the characters in these nine short stories do not speak with my own voice. First, they are the voice of the narrator of the story and second they are the voice in your mind that you give them.

I want to keep it that way. Believe me, those that know me and have read some of these stories either say, *Where did Erik come up with that idea?* Or, *That story sounds like one Erik would tell after a couple of beers.* And the very worst one of all is, *Which character am I?*

Yet, I feel a necessity to introduce myself and to give you some guidance before you journey through these nine stories. No, I will not break the cardinal rule of *explaining* a story – a story should after all be *told*. But there are significant things about each story that must be addressed. I pondered the idea of putting a little narrative at the end of each story but I knew I would get carried away – as I may here.

First, let me answer the one question I get asked the most. Why a book of short stories? They don't sell, people say. Novels are what publishers (and agents) want. Well, because I love the genre of short fiction. If you want my list of author's that have impressed me then here we go: Ambrose Bierce writer of "An Occurrence at Owl Creek Bridge"; "The Lady and the Tiger" by Aslan; Anton Chekov; Shirley Jackson's "The Lottery"; Bernard Malamud; Samuel Taylor Coleridge (yes, I know he's a poet); Eudora Welty and Mary Shelly, just to name a few... all you Stephen King lovers.

Now before you start yelling, *Plagiarist!* I point out that these authors impressed me but if you want to split hairs I will. *Jurassic Park?* A re-telling of the before mentioned Mary Shelly's *Frankenstein*. *Star Wars* (the first one from the seventies)? Homer's *Odyssey* told by the point of view by Telemakhos. Obi Wan? Athena. I can go on and on if you like but let's move to these stories, please.

I have nine short stories that do need a little explaining since they span some time and have certain meaning. For example, *Black Stone* is actually a short story submitted in a twenty-four hour contest where I was given a theme of a psychic convention and only 850 words to use. I began the story three hours before the deadline and it was simply marred with errors that I have since fixed.

A Pock of Lips is of course a parody of the *Apocalypse Now* movie with one added ingredient. I've been criticized for verb tense problems in that story but if you look at the list of authors I named above, you may find something.

Oh, and most importantly, I believe that each of my stories – and this is why I love short fiction – is Life en Medes Res. In my opinion, too many writers start their short stories like *Penthouse Letters*. You know, *I can't believe I'm writing this* or *If you are the unfortunate soul who is reading this...* You know what I mean. Take my story *Lullaby* for instance. Point of view is skewed in my world and *you* must decide if you want to continue to follow something where you have no control over the outcome. Think of them as an out of body experience where you get a short glimpse into someone else's life.

I also owe many thanks to many people, so many that I can't name them without taking up twenty pages and leaving someone out. But thanks to my friends, family and writing and editing peers.

Finally, with so many riddles I love to insert in my stories I leave you simply with this one. The curse of *The Scarlet Ibis* is finally lifted.

Erik Schumann

July 1, 2003

I dreamt again,
Of the warrior poet
I dreamt of riding a great steed into great battle
With great smoke and cannon thunder
I was numb from the tears of the poppy plant

Alas, I awoke to a world...
A world with no stirruped warriors...

What of poets you ask?
Alas, that is for you to decide
Decided by what you read...
And by your own tears

- Anonymous

Tomorrow, and tomorrow, and tomorrow,
Creeps in this petty pace from day to day,
To the last syllable of recorded time;
And all are yesterdays have lighted fools
The way to dusty death. Out, out, brief candle!
Life's but a walking shadow; a poor player,
That struts and frets his hour upon the stage,
And then is heard no more: it is a tale
Told by an idiot, full of sound of fury,
Signifying nothing.

Macbeth
-William Shakespeare

Tomorrow and Tomorrow

It was a new day, that was for sure but the weather this Wednesday was the same as the last three days: hot, humid and all-around miserable. At 7:45 in the morning it was already eighty degrees. For Patrick Ostrah it was just a workday, another morning battling rush hour traffic and surviving the morning radio shows.

Patrick Ostrah eased into his old, foreign, midsized car just as he did every weekday morning. He glanced over to his next-door neighbor, Mrs. Ashton, who was dragging her plastic garbage can, which had no wheels, down the driveway to the street. He waved neighborly to her and smiled. She lifted her free hand and awkwardly waved back as the trash can skip behind her, jolting the lid off. Patrick smiled once more and said he was sorry for making her lose the lid. Mrs. Ashton waved him off and wished Patrick a good day.

Once in his car, Patrick closed the car door. His car greeted him by running the seatbelt from the front part of the door, down the track that ran along the top of the window and locked into place, as it did every morning.

In the passenger seat rested his laptop – in its case – as well as some folders containing reports and other papers for several different projects Patrick was working on. The folders actually fit into one of the pockets of the laptop case. Underneath the laptop case was another hard plastic case. Inside this case was his stainless steel .38 caliber Taurus handgun, with a four-inch barrel. He bought the gun several years ago for Kelly, when Patrick started traveling occasionally. Kelly, actually didn't care for it that much and had only gone to the gun range a couple of times with Patrick. She didn't mind owning it and would use it if she had to – which she knew how to do – but she didn't enjoy going to the range like Patrick did. Patrick really wanted a .44 or .45 caliber gun but it was too much money for the couple right now and too much gun for Kelly, so he stuck with the little .38.

Patrick had a permit to carry the gun concealed and loaded. Loaded it was.

Sitting next to the gun case, under the laptop case, were Patrick's ear plugs in their own case and his protective eyeglasses that the range made a shooter wear.

The engine turned over without incident, as it did every morning. The radio came to life with the car; he never turned it off with the car so there was no surprise there. The morning crew on the radio was in full swing, degrading some caller trying to win tickets to an upcoming concert or something. The clock on the dashboard of his car read 7:47. The radio program would be announcing last night's lottery numbers in three minutes. He had bought five numbers the night before; the jackpot was up to seventy million dollars. He only played when the jackpot got high, like seventy million, and he had one set of numbers consisting of birthdays and other special numbers that he always played and then he would but four more sets of numbers that the lottery machine picked at random. So he had five sets of numbers; he would have to get all six numbers right to win the jackpot.

He opened the middle console of his car where he kept the ticket, along with a pack of Camel Lights and a lighter. He pulled the ticket out and placed it on top of his laptop case. When they read the numbers over the radio, if he was stopped at a light, he could at least glance and see how he did.

He yawned as he pulled his car out of his neighborhood. He had been up late the night before working on his novel. He was almost done. He didn't expect to make any money or anything off it, it was just a goal he set and he wanted to complete it. Besides, he and his wife, Kelly lived in a small ranch-style house in a quaint neighborhood. The house was old, with three bedrooms, all sharing one bathroom at the end of the hall. Kelly and Patrick obviously shared the master bedroom. Across the hall, and to the right of the bathroom was the guestroom, though they had few guests that spent the night. The third bedroom was next to the guestroom and was, more or less a junk room, filled with unused workout equipment, boxes of books and other useless things that they felt they could not throw out. The kitchen and living room were both small, but the couple had built a little nook off of the living room, complete with computer, printer, etc. It was here, in the nook, where Kelly had been spending her evenings studying and writing papers for her finals.

When Kelly was studying in the nook that meant no television for Patrick. He, instead, retreated to the guestroom where there was a small desk that gave him enough room to open his laptop and work on his novel.

Such was how last night went.

Leaving his neighborhood he noticed the people sitting on the street corner or sitting on the bench that marked the bus stop. The fact that Patrick made a right turn out of his neighborhood and that the bus stop was on his right, gave him a good view of the people waiting. Since Patrick went this way every day he recognized some of the faces waiting for the eight o'clock bus. There was one woman sitting on the bench now that Patrick had seen almost daily. The woman's face was partially covered by a hardback book she was reading. Patrick could see the author's glossy portrait on the back. Oh, thought, Patrick, it was *him*. The woman made brief eye contact with Patrick then returned to the pages of her book.

How odd, thought Patrick. She rides the bus every day, surely to save money, yet she buys a hardback. Patrick shook his head. Then he thought of the way she dismissed him. *A simple glance!* Oh, I'm sure if I was what's-his-face – the author of the book, the book would've been down and she would have been telling everybody at the bus stop who just drove by. *Everybody! Everybody!* She would shout. *Patrick Ostrah just drove by. Here his picture is on the cover of my hardback.* That is what she would say. Maybe when his novel is done.

"Gee zus!" Shouted Patrick as he slammed on his brakes. He had been watching the people at the bus stop so long out the passenger window he did not see that the truck in front of him had stopped. He barely missed rear-ending the dented piece of crap. Three Mexican workers were sitting in the back of the truck with their backs lined against the cab. They were laughing uncontrollably.

Patrick looked out the passenger window towards the bus stop. Everyone was laughing, except for the woman reading the book. She had the book in her lap and was shaking her head. She turned to someone to her left and Patrick thought he could read her lips. *That's why I take the bus every day because idiots like him don't know how to drive* is what Patrick thought he read her lips say.

Every day.

That's right, old woman, thought Patrick, *every day.* He was checking his mirrors to get around the truck hauling the laughing three amigos. He zipped around it with no problem. The dashboard clock read 7:50. Shit! They were giving the winning lottery numbers. Patrick looked to his right, in the passenger seat. The ticket was gone. With a quick glance he saw it on the floorboard, out of reach, along with his laptop. Only his gun in its case remained in the seat; everything else was on the floorboard from when he slammed on his brakes.

The guy on the radio was spewing the numbers out one after another. The ticket was overturned so Patrick couldn't read the numbers anyway.

"Damn!" Patrick yelled to himself. He figured he could get the numbers off the Internet once he got to work. He could also check out what happened in the news since he had no access to the TV last night.

Patrick knew that it didn't matter. He hadn't won. It was just a dream. In fact, he called it his F.U. dream. In the F.U. dream Patrick wins the lottery and gets to tell everyone he despises to F.U.! His boss, Mr. Vinson, was at the top of the list. Oh, Patrick would give it to him good. There were others but Vinson was at the top; then, after he had told the world to go to hell, he and Kelly would go for an around the world vacation – damn the economy and world order! They would hit every tropical paradise in the world and walk hand-in-hand to sunsets all over the world.

F. U. to the world – middle finger extended!

But, Patrick knew his odds of winning were as good as being struck by lightning, so every day it was the same routine, same route, same time. Time. A simple measurement, thought Patrick, that mankind has devised to mark events past, present and future. But it seemed to Patrick that one day just melted into the next. His activities at work, at home – hell even the route he took to work; it was the same today as it was yesterday and would be tomorrow and the next day and the next.

Patrick's mind drifted for a moment. At first he had the feeling like he was forgetting something as he slowly crept through Atlanta traffic. Ah, he thought, and he quickly opened the middle console of the car that separated the driver's seat from the passenger's seat. Within a few seconds he had produced a Camel Light cigarette and his lighter. He lit it and was once again forced to hit the brakes hard again when the car in front of him suddenly stopped.

He banged the steering wheel with the palms of his hands and took a deep drag from the cigarette. He cracked the window about two inches and blew the smoke out into the hot, hazy, humid Atlanta air. The dashboard clock now read 8:04. *Tomorrow and tomorrow and tomorrow*, he thought to himself. What was that from? A poem? Something Kelly had read to him perhaps?

8:05. Shit! It usually took an hour to get to work, which meant he should be pulling into the parking lot at eight forty-five. But traffic was horrible this morning. And today, waiting in the office, there was some client in from Chicago. Flew in last night. Patrick was prepared for the meeting, had his PowerPoint presentation all ready. Mr. Vinson would no doubt be up his ass all day and if he were late; if Patrick Ostrah was late today with a client from Chicago in town Mr. Vinson would unleash Armageddon into Patrick Ostrah's life. At least that's how Patrick's imagination drew up the scenario.

Patrick was not one of those people that were late all the time or called in sick – hell he hadn't called in sick for the six years he had been with the company. In fact, thought Patrick, he had not taken time off for a vacation since... when? Since two years ago when he and Kelly drove to Florida for the Fourth of July. And this year's Independence Day past a month ago!

There would be no vacation this summer or this year, not with Kelly taking classes summer and autumn. *Tomorrow and tomorrow and tomorrow creeps at this petty pace...* like Atlanta rush-hour traffic. Tomorrow and tomorrow, there would be work and more work. There would be Mr. Vinson and more Mr. Vinson.

Mr. Vinson. That soulless son-of-a-bitch. Patrick had been with the company six years now – going on seven. That was nearly two years longer than Patrick's Five Year Plan where he told himself that he would work at this company, for Mr. Vinson for five years, gain experience, then move on. Nearly, seven years now and Patrick hadn't even looked to find a new job, not in this economy. And the novel he started in college remained unfinished. The two pages a day he promised to write, went... where? Patrick had no answer, except unwritten.

He threw the spent cigarette through the crack of the car window.

"C'mon!" shouted Patrick and he slammed his palms on the steering wheel again. "What is the hold-up?" He glanced up through his windshield and saw a news helicopter speed by through the air and Patrick cursed it for how free it flew above the congestion. He extended his middle finger, "Put this on the news, you bastard."

His gesture caught the attention of the guy driving a mail truck to his left. Patrick could see the mailman clearly since the truck's steering wheel was on the right side of the vehicle. The mailman was decked out in his little short pants and was laughing at Patrick's tantrum. Oh sure, thought Patrick, you guys are the ones that go nuts and shoot-up every place and you're laughing at me?

He lit another Camel Light.

Traffic moved... for the lane the mail truck was in and the laughing mailman pulled away.

Idiot, thought Patrick as the mailman drove off. *Tale told by an idiot.* Yes! That is part of the, the soliloquy from that damn play, thought Patrick. Which one, though? His lane started to move. And more than a few feet! Maybe it was over. Maybe there had been a wreck that they just now cleared. Patrick looked out into the Atlanta sky again. It *was* a beautiful morning. Yes, there was some haze, of course, but the sky was a clear blue dome with only sparse, transparent clouds. This was not just an ordinary day, he thought. Nope, not with a sky and morning this grand, no matter how many times a man sees it.

Damn! Traffic stopped again. He finished that cigarette and threw it out the window, then counted five more left in the pack. He shook one up to his mouth, pulled it out of the pack with his lips then lit it.

An orange sign on the right side of the road warned drivers to reduce speed, spelled out in flashing yellow light bulbs. Another Department of Transportation sign was just past that one. His car inched forward; the sign was coming into view. The flashing yellow lights on this DOT trailer pulsed like a heartbeat, making an arrow, directing drivers to merge left.

So this is the hold-up. The DOT has decided to do roadwork during morning rush hour traffic. Perfect. Just perfect.

8:26 the dashboard clock pulsed. Patrick looked at his wristwatch. The hands nearly matched the dashboard clock time. The road will widen at the river, he decided. He wasn't going to be late; he would be there just in time for his nine o'clock meeting.

But what if he *was* late? Patrick let his mind wander. Well, first Mr. Vinson might patronize Patrick by dropping a hint that he was late. Vinson might even say that *they would talk about it later... in his office.* That damn office where Vinson all ways makes *you* close the door behind you.

Vinson wanted to see you nervous, wanted everyone outside the closed door to whisper and to wonder your fate.

Damn it! Why isn't traffic moving?!

During his daydreaming he hadn't paid one ounce of attention to the radio. If quizzed he couldn't say what happened or what songs were played. All for the best, he thought, he didn't want any stupid songs stuck in his head. He all ready had that soliloquy thing running through his head. It kept nagging at him. Tomorrow and tomorrow and something about an idiot strutting and fretting his stuff, he thought. He then became acutely aware that the Rolling Stones were on the radio. That's it! *Macbeth.* Shakespeare was talking about Mick Jagger! Patrick laughed out loud at the thought.

He quickly stopped laughing though when he turned to look to the car next to him. The man in the Lexus was gingerly lifting a cup of hot coffee to his lips. Steam rose from the convenience store cup. Patrick watched as the man took a sip then winced.

Shit! Patrick realized he had forgot to stop for his own cup of coffee this morning. All this traffic and daydreaming about a William Shakespeare something or other and he forgot to stop for his morning coffee. That wasn't usual. Patrick all ways stopped for coffee; none of that office crap for him. Oh, this day was starting out bad.

And why have we not moved?

He had another cigarette, just to calm the nerves. It didn't help.

From under the hood there came what Patrick could only describe as a *clacking* noise. Then? Then, Patrick put a hand up to one of the air conditioner vents. The air got warmer and warmer. He looked at the car's temperature gauge; it was beginning steadily to rise. He quickly turned the A/C off.

He flicked it back on and traffic began to move at the same time. The air coming out of the vents was not cool, but at least the car's temperature gauge stopped rising.

C'mon. Keep moving traffic. Oh, Patrick was beginning to sweat. He rolled down his window for a moment but the heat outside was oppressive. It appeared to Patrick that as long as the car was moving, it wasn't overheating and the A/C was a breeze, if a only a warm one.

Traffic stopped.

Now what?! Patrick glanced at the clock on the dashboard; it read 8:43. Fifteen minutes, that's all he had. And now the air blowing on his face was growing hotter. The temperature gauge on the car was rising, along with Patrick's temper. Sweat crowned his brow but he could feel his whole body beginning to break out in sweat. He wasn't going to make it. He was going to be late. He lifted himself from his seat and tried to look over the automobiles ahead of him. He couldn't see anything but he could feel his back drenched in sweat.

He moved fifty feet and the clock read 8:50. *You're going to be late. You're going to be late and Mr.Vinson's going to be there waiting with the client from Chicago, tapping his foot and looking at his watch, shaking his head. And once you do show up and after you meet with your client – who you've kept waiting – Vinson's going to call you into his office, ask you to close the door behind you and have a seat in that chair in front of his desk. You know the chair; it's the one you fidgeted in during your interview and the one you fidget in every time you have your annual review.* This was the scenario Patrick's mind gave him. Of course, Patrick knew he was overreacting. He knew it. He also knew that flying on a commercial jet was infinitely safer than driving his car. But he also never needed three fingers of whiskey to get in a car like he needed before boarding any airplane.

8:53. A stalled car.

A fricking stalled car was what was holding up traffic. Patrick passed it and the traffic congestion lightened. But, Patrick knew he was still going to be late for work. "I swear to God, Vinson," Patrick said out loud. "I swear to God if you give me one rash of shit I'm going to kick your ass in front of the almighty client from Chicago." The car was still running hot and wisps of steam were now slipping and curling their way through the vents and openings in the hood. This filled Patrick with a sense of dread as well as rising anger. He did not want to be like the stalled car he just past. "Have to keep the car moving," he whispered to himself between teeth that were beginning to clinch. Patrick was coming to an intersection where he needed to make a left turn. The lane was moving now and he was in line to go. Go!

"This left and cut down past the river," he said to himself. He was sure traffic would be light and he would have a straight shot to the office. He would deal with Vinson when he got there. He didn't need to glance at the passenger seat. He knew what was there.

He lit another cigarette.

In front of him now was a Ryder truck, blocking his view. He was nearing the intersection, he knew, but he could not see the color of the light. He needed to make the left. If he stopped, the car might overheat. If the truck goes, I'm going he thought.

The Ryder truck went and made the left turn. Patrick followed.

The light was yellow. The car in the left lane of oncoming traffic was slowing for the light. The Ryder truck accelerated and put some distance between it and Patrick.

Patrick accelerated as well to make the left turn... and there it was – a dump truck. It was red with the word MACK spelled out across the grill in chrome letters. It was in the right lane of oncoming traffic and had accelerated like

Patrick to make the light. Patrick never saw it until now. On the hood was as ornament of what Patrick concluded in a split second was a bulldog. The truck was barreling down on him. There may have been a screech of tires. God, the steel bumper on this thing was huge. Two red flags were on either side of the bumper, torn and flapping in the wind.

Then the impact.

It was as if the car itself exploded as the mammoth truck ate up Patrick's mid-sized aluminum import. There were no air bags deployed for safety – the car was too old. There was nothing but a dashboard folding, a shattering windshield and a crumpling hood clawing its way towards an unprotected Patrick. For Patrick, it felt like his teeth were torn from his gums on impact as his head whipped forward, then snapped back. The real pain was in his legs. The front of the car and dash was biting down on his legs, a combination of metal and plastic gnawing its way up his body.

Patrick's car, obviously, was knocked backwards. How far, Patrick couldn't tell but almost as quickly as the truck hit him, the back of his car impacted with something else. In the second that it happened, Patrick could only conclude it was another vehicle. The world spun out of control for both an instant and an eternity. The sound of metal grinding on asphalt and broken glass was all Patrick heard until his car came to rest.

He wasn't sure if he was conscious or not. His body was washed with pain. Neck, legs, head, he only knew that he wasn't dead, yet – there was too much pain. The world was dark but through the darkness he could smell the scent of burnt rubber and gasoline. Gasoline?

He fought the pain and the darkness. His mind was trying to shut down, to shield Patrick from the pain. But he fought and light flickered through the darkness as he opened his eyes. Everything was a blur, but the world began to come back to him. He was aware now of his surroundings. He was in his car, upside down and trapped. His tie lay across his face and brushed his face with something wet and sticky. Blood. The steering wheel was against his chest. He couldn't see his legs; the car had devoured them. He was cold and trembling. How could it be so cold on a hot day, he thought. The answer came quickly to him. *Because you're dying, stupid, that's why.* He whimpered at the thought. He was scared and wanted out. He wanted out that instant! How did this happen? If only I had stopped for coffee. If only I had stopped at the light. If only the car was not running hot. If only the guy from Chicago…

In an instant it seemed like all the yesterdays were flooding from this pain racked mind. And with each thought, he kept thinking, *I could have done something different, something!* He couldn't believe this is what his life came to. This, and no more.

He screamed as people began rushing to his car. A man in a suit was at his broken window, looking in, his eyes filled with horror. "Are… are you all right?" The man asked in a dry voice that cracked with fear.

"No," Patrick said, trying to stay calm. "I'm in a great deal of pain." The words came out as if from a child, soft and lacking confidence. In a different circumstance Patrick may have said something like *Fuck no, you idiot, look at me! My organs are being pushed out my ass like sausage through a grinder!* But then again, Patrick never was dying before. "I'm cold. I'm hurt…. I'm dying," he said.

Patrick heard people screaming from the street. He heard footsteps as people rushed towards his car. He heard a woman yelling that she was a nurse. The good samaritan that had first appeared was pulling on Patrick's left arm, trying to free him. Past that man, Patrick saw the bare legs of a mailman running up to the car. Through blurred eyes he saw a woman standing, almost frozen, her hands covering her mouth; her eyes were wide in dismay. It reminded Patrick of the woman he saw at the bus stop earlier.

You dumbass; you're holding up traffic, Patrick thought to himself. He knew someone late to work was thinking that now. Someone like him. That is what I would say, he thought. Instead, he whimpered, "I'm dying."

The man trying to free him gave little comfort. "No you're not," the man said. But neither the man nor Patrick believed it.

"Is he alive?" It was a woman's voice.

"Yes," spoke the man.

Patrick thought he heard a helicopter hovering in the air and the faint sound of sirens in the distance. Good luck getting through traffic, Patrick thought. He was going unconscious now but he heard someone yell, "It's on fire! Oh my God it's on fire!"

The tugs on Patrick's arm became more vigorous as smoke danced in front of Patrick's eyes, circling and twisting into the Atlanta summer air. Great puffs filled the inside of the car as well.

"Does anyone have a fire extinguisher?!" shouted someone. Patrick thought he heard the swooshing noise of a fire extinguisher, but instead someone was pulling the samaritan away from Patrick.

"Don't leave me," Patrick whined with a dry throat.

It was too late. Everyone that had rushed to help was now running to save themselves. No summer vacation this year. *No walks with Kelly on the beach; someone else would have that honor at some point – along with many more.* "NO! NO!" Patrick screamed. "HELP ME!"

Patrick saw his parents weeping at his grave. He saw Mr. Vinson shaking the hand of a new employee. He saw a lot of things in the span of less than a minute. He thought back at the woman on the sidewalk, her hands covering her mouth in disbelief. She was in shock now, but later she would be retelling all her friends about *seeing the idiot burnt up today in rush hour traffic trying to make a light.*

"Don't let me die. I DON'T WANT TO DIE!" Patrick Ostrah screamed the words loud and with fury – a man making his last gasp in front of the public as a curtain of fire fell.

All While the Gods Watched

All while the gods watched I moved from shadow to shadow within the house the gods had set as my stage. The place was silent except for a clock in the living room that ticked and ticked, second to second – moving much slower than my beating heart.

I paused in the foyer and looked up the staircase. I waited I guess for some sign from the gods, some intervention... but none came. I felt as if I and I alone were awake in the world – *alive* in the world! Everything was set for my bidding and the gods' amusement.

I must confess I do not feel as if my actions were my own. Numerous times before that night I had thought and planned about what was going to happen; and never, never did I believe any thoughts to be my own. All was planned and prepared by the gods for their enjoyment. I was – *am* today this day – merely a character in their ghastly game.

I even remember when I purchased the knife that I carried that night. When I bought it I remember thinking about the clerk selling me the dagger; he must know what I am planning; he is perhaps the author of this play, or perhaps he is a mere character like me. In the store I felt like winking at the clerk when he sold me the blade, but that would have been out of place – out of... character.

I counted eleven steps that lead to the prize. I remember thinking, how many times have I done this? How many more times will I have to? The gods did nothing to slow my pace up the stairs. They were probably as eager as I, to see what waited, for they surely did not slow my pace. Yet, I felt, as I do know, that the watching gods could walk away and leave me in limbo at any time and return at any time to make me continue my actions. Why? For their pleasure?

The first door on the left was the first that I entered. When I did, I found myself free of inhibitions. I gave myself completely to the moment. With one long plunge of the knife, I relieved the sleeping cherub from the bounds of this earth.

I wondered if the gods were amused or appalled. Either way they did not stop me. I have concluded that they cannot see in the future. No, they force me to act but never stop me, no matter how horrific my actions. They must watch and I must act. In fact, I question my own existence; though I know the gods are real. But just how real I don't know... and I fear neither do they. Perhaps *they* answer to a higher power as well.

But back to that night, I went as the gods instructed, room-to-room of the house like some mechanical man, for I had no feelings, no remorse given to me by the gods. Every room was empty and then I came to the last... the master bedroom. The door was closed but *that* room was full of energy, like electricity. It was pouring from the room through the closed door. Every hair on my body stood on end. There was, I must admit, a moment of apprehension, maybe one the gods did not expect as I twisted the knob to the room. What if it is locked? I thought. Would the gods do this? No. I felt *this* room held *the* prize. I turned the knob and it was unlocked! And the door opened without so much as a creak or a squeak.

All was dark, but my eyes had already adjusted from the moment I entered the house. I moved like a phantom, not a noise made. I could see but one ruffled mound in a bed made for two. I took a moment to look around the room that was bathed in blue, shadowy moonlight. There was a nightstand with a clock and a lamp on it; the numbers were red; the time the clock read was and is meaningless.

I moved now with purpose. This was it. I could feel the energy. *The climax was now near.* There was but one person fast asleep in the bed. I squinted to see any features. A she. I knew it would be! It had to be! For, shall I say, the gods' sake! I could see her hair and the features of the woman. I could hear her delicate breathing; I was close enough to see the blanket rise and fall. I was so close, close enough to touch the warm flesh. She stirred. And then like an alarm, an explosion, the sleeping beauty burst from the covers, screaming!

Imagine my shock.

I nearly had a heart attack, nearly dropped my knife. I could not comprehend. I knew there needed to be silence. And I also became very aware of something else: Some of the gods wanted her to kill *me*! I could and can feel their feelings. They have led me here. I don't even know my name! I have done their bidding, only asking questions! I have done everything they have asked *but I do know that I am alive.* And I simply won't just die! Not even for gods! She was fighting the covers to come after me, screaming. The screaming. I knew there needed to be silence. Silence!

I thrust my knife, again and again, tearing, shredding, cutting, stabbing until there was no more screaming, only silence. *Hate to disappoint some of you,* I thought. All I heard now was my own heartbeat and the pounding in my head where the screams were still echoing but fading. My face was close to hers. My warm breath touching her cheek. I don't know why but I reached for the lamp on the nightstand and clicked it on.

It was then that I saw the horror. The absolute horror of what I had done. The gods, now while they watched, squinted to see what they made me do! But I know they don't want to see all of it, some have already had enough.

The woman was beautiful – no lovely. In an instant I was in love and within the same moment I was grief-stricken. How cruel! How absolutely cruel to love and... and then to lose it without knowing. My... my actions were not my own.

I then thought of the child in the other room. What had I done? What had the gods made me do?

And now her beauty haunts me. I kept a lock of her hair. All while the gods watched better to have loved and lost, then never to have loved at all...

All while the gods watched I moved from shadow to shadow...

Thanksgiving At Sugar Loaf

The conversation with his grandson from the airport was light and brisk. Now, they headed north, up Interstate 85, just north of Atlanta. The car moved fast along the interstate. It moved quiet and smooth, continuing northbound. After all it was a luxury car, one of the high-end Acura models. Ivan "Bud" Velnik knew Honda made these luxury cars... but he didn't care. Mitsubishi made the Zeros that raised hell in the Pacific theatre and now they made cars and televisions and all sorts of other stuff. None of it bothered Bud – not like it bothered some of Bud's old buddies.

At his age now, Bud had more than his fair share of time to reflect on both peace and war. The few things that Bud realized, for himself anyway, is in war there is no time for philosophy. There are few times for mercy. There are few times for reflection; and often times you wanted to put things out of your mind and not remember a damned thing anyway. In battle, civilized humanity slips away from a young man viciously and violently.

An image Bud always carried with him – before, during and after the war – was that of his mother tucking him into bed at night when he was a child. It was warm; it was safe. You would say your prayers to God, praying only for the best for the world. And you were safe, without fear and without hate.

But in battle, in war, all that's gone, and for many it's gone at an early age – so damn young, Bud often thought. Bud could remember seeing the young dead boys, their bodies half covered in ponchos. Some of the young faces of the dead Marines Bud saw looked like they had just been tucked in by their mother for one final goodnight. In fact, Bud thought that was why so many dying boys cried out for their mothers and for home. Those screams and scenes scarred his soul like no other.

Nevertheless, wars end and Bud found that peace and humanity is easily lost in battle but not easily regained in civilian life even after a "good war" like World War II. Yet, Bud found humanity and peace in some ways. To Bud, war was like a living nightmare, one where you cannot scream yourself awake, even though you try, and one where your mother cannot comfort you even though you cry out. It is a horror that must be lived and dealt with.

Afterwards, you can awake from the nightmares. If you live, you can come home. You can't bring back your buddies, or act more valiantly, or chase away the nightmares, but no one raises any more tombstones in the nightmares, either. So, Bud learned to live with what he saw and what he did and during the days he lived his life after the war he lived it as positive as he could. The nights sometimes brought its nightmares. Even during the day sometimes, the hairs on his neck would stand and he would think all too vividly of a lost buddy... or two. Nonetheless, as the years passed, he raised a family and had a career as a high school History teacher. He regained his life and it had been a good one. And here he was now, riding along with his grandson in his grandson's luxury sedan to his grandson's luxury house to spend Thanksgiving with his beloved family.

Bud had no reason as to why the thought of the war had come to his mind and then left so fast. Probably, just... who knows? Oh yes, the foreign car they were riding in... the Japanese-made luxury car.

"We're almost there now, Grampa," relayed his grandson. Bud remembered the street name his grandson, Jake, lived on was Weatherstone. He remembered it from all the letters Jake's wife, Helen wrote. They were always nice cards and letters that Helen sent, always accompanied with pictures of the family. The twins were what, seven now? The boy in his teens? Some things were hard for Bud to remember, other things he couldn't forget in a lifetime.

A green highway sign was quickly coming into view. Bud squinted his eyes a bit to try to read it better.

SUGAR LOAF HILL 6 MARINE DIVISION

That was how Bud read it from its original distance.

Sugar Loaf?

A chill ran down Bud. All that thinking of the war, he thought.

The car drew closer. Bud almost did not want to look; his palms were sweating. He glanced up.

SUGAR LOAF PKWY NEXT EXIT

He had simply read it wrong the first time. The car sped by the sign and onto the off ramp. The rest of the way Bud and Jake exchanged small talk, mainly about sports, Bud's health and of course, Bud coming to live with Jake and his family. Passing the large houses put Bud's mind at some ease that there would be room for him. These houses were mansions! "Here we are," said Jake as he pulled the car into a steep driveway that led up to a huge brick house. A mini-van was parked on the left so Jake took his place to the right of it.

It was warm for late November and as Bud stepped out of the car he saw Helen was standing with the front door wide open. She had a wide, genuine smile on her face and she was waving.

Bud's aged body ached as he stepped out and by the time he had the car door closed Helen had made it from the front steps and was hugging Bud. "Oh, it's great to see you Dad," she said, her hug growing tighter as she spoke. She loosened her grip and kissed the old man on the cheek. Her smile never left her face and her eyes were bright. She's as sincere as a person gets, thought Bud. She doesn't put on a show in front of people then speak ill behind their back. Bud knew that when Jake and Helen had talked about him coming now for Thanksgiving and possibly for, well longer that Helen was sincere in her approval; hell, the idea may have come from her.

As far as Bud was concerned all the Velnik men had married well. Bud had married his high school sweetheart, Alma, in 1943 when he was eighteen. He married her right before he shipped-off – and she was all ready carrying their son. She made Bud promise to enlist in the Navy and indeed he tried; but when he was at the recruiter's office, the officer in charge said, "Welcome to the Marines" and put Bud's file in the Marine stack. At least that is how Bud always told the story.

Bud's son, Robert, was born in late November 1943. In fact his birthday would have been a week earlier to the day. Robert and his lovely wife, Pamela, died in a car wreck back in 1983. Pamela survived the initial crash and Bud held her hand when she died – Pamela's parents were two hours too late.

Fourteen years earlier Bud held the hand of Alma as cancer took her life. How many dying hands had Bud held? Too many. But now he was breaking from the loving embrace of his grandson's wife.

After Robert and Pamela died Jake came to live with Bud – thank God he hadn't been in the car that New Year's Eve night of the wreck. Jake grew into manhood under Bud's guidance. And in Bud's opinion, he had raised the boy all right. Jake could've easily became a rebellious, angry teen, but he had done all right and Bud was sure Jake had fun along the way – had enjoyed the years of his youth in spite of the loss of his parents.

Bud did not run his home like a military boot camp. The way Bud saw it, he was an American citizen who did his duty for his country then came home and worked and raised a family, although it was a small family. Robert was the only son he and Alma had; the pregnancy had been difficult. But the family had always been a close one, filled with love. The hug from Helen was a testament to how close the family really was, even down through the generations.

Jake removed Bud's luggage from the car and placed everything in the driveway. "Let me help you," said Bud.

"No, I got it," he said with a slight strain.

The three walked towards the front of the house, moving at the pace that Bud's body allowed. Helen rubbed a hand tenderly up and down Bud's back. Bud had a jacket on for the November weather; otherwise Helen would've no doubt felt the scars that healed nearly sixty years ago in a Guam hospital. Helen leaned into Bud, like a daughter into a father. "Was there much traffic at the airport," she asked.

"No," replied Jake proudly; speaking across Bud to Helen since Bud walked in the middle of the three. "Tomorrow will be the busiest day of travel all year. Today was not too bad." Bud had flown in on the Tuesday before Thanksgiving and Jake was right, the experience wasn't a bad one.

"Well, Dad, we're just so glad you're here," chimed Helen. "The kids will be home from school soon and I know they're looking forward to seeing you. Today is their last day before the holidays." Thanksgiving was two days away but the house, especially around the kitchen, was filled with delightful scents for Tuesday night's dinner. Dinner was some type of pot roast, Bud guessed, and vegetables and other delicious side dishes.

To an outsider, thought Bud, Helen might appear, or even be described by some fool, as one of those vacuous soccer moms. But Jake met Helen in college and Helen was by far the better student. It just so happens, that by nature, it is the women that must carry the child. And like most Velniks, children followed soon after marriage. Helen had a degree in Math and worked as an actuary (which was difficult to believe due to her extroverted personality, Bud all ways thought) but found that her love for her children far outweighed her love for her career. The couple was lucky enough that Jake's career could support the whole family, so she sacrificed her career to raise her children. It was a decision she never regretted but one she said she knew others rolled their eyes at.

Bud was one that did not roll his eyes. In his mind he had married a tough broad in Alma, so had his son and grandson. Bud had concluded many years ago that people with agendas, that people with self-serving ambitions, and in this day and age people with time on their hands rarely acknowledged those who sacrifice. And Helen had sacrificed. Her family was *her* life. How her children turned out as adults would surely be determined more by Helen's presence than by some big deal closed on the golf course by Jake. Both were crucial to the family survival, but which had sacrificed the most?

Just then the front door exploded open as two young twin girls bolted into the house! "Is he here?! Is he here?!" They screamed. As soon as they saw him they dropped their book bags and papers. "Grampa!" they screamed. Grampa, is how they knew Bud. They called Helen's father, Papa. Bud knelt and took one in each arm. Hugs and kisses and hugs and kisses. Bud's mind wandered nowhere from the moment. No, time had passed and nearly sixty years of living quiets the ghosts but it doesn't silence them; they skulk around in the memory knowing exactly the right time to yell, *Boo!*

They had already rattled their chains once with the road sign.

"Grampa, look what we drew today in class," spoke one of the twins. It had been so long that Bud did not know which spoke the words until he saw both girls hold up similar pictures. Each of them had made a turkey from tracing their hand. He took each girls picture, stood up with some reluctance from his back. He held the pictures out in front of him. His glasses would have helped but he could make out each scribbled bird. In the top left corner of each picture a name was also etched. He read the names silently then looked to the small girl that first addressed him. "Well," Bud said, "that looks like a real turkey, Dana." He then turned to the other little girl. "And so does yours, Ursy! In fact, they look almost identical," he laughed.

Dana and Ursusla were their names, although the family called Ursula, named after Helen's grandmother, Ursy. Bud glanced over to Helen and Jake who were watching from the kitchen. The couple nodded to the old man on the clever way he could tell the girls apart.

The girls were dressed differently and Dana had longer hair. Bud knew they liked being twins but they also liked to be recognized for their individuality. For the rest of Bud's visit it would be easy to tell them apart; they even dressed differently.

Except…

Their sneakers were the same.

Suddenly, those old ghosts, woven in the cobwebs of old memories rattled. Bud was injured on May 15, 1945. It was the fourth day out of the nine days that the Marines had tried to take that small hill dubbed Sugar Loaf. Bud never saw what hit him but he was convinced that it was the bullets from a nambu gun. He was hit up his whole left side, from his left thigh up in to his upper chest – he had almost lost his left arm. But he was still one of the lucky ones. He had made it to the back lines where he could receive medical attention; there were many Marines that spent the night wounded, under constant attack on Sugar Loaf. There were few foxholes but many shell holes where a man could try to fit his eyes and ass in his helmet when the mortars and shelling fell. The Japanese turned mortar fire into a deadly art form. In fact, when Bud did make it back to what was considered the command post he knew he still was not safe. The enemy had taken out officers planning an assault on Sugar Loaf that were gathered too close in an observation post that was supposedly out of harm's way. But that was as far as Bud could go injured.

But what the ghosts of his memory were whispering now was *The boots. Look at their boots.* The vision was all too clear. He was lying in the mud, waiting for a corpsman. Just lying there, in the middle of, of... that memory's unclear; Bud was in some shock. But the view across the way, he remembers, the bodies stacked up and covered by ponchos. They were stacked like wood, their booted feet exposed – those bodies that still had legs. Bud remembered looking at that pile of dead men and those stacked boots. He looked down at his own feet. His boots were the same as the dead men.

"Dad? Dad? Are you all right?" It was Helen at Bud's side now, a look of concern on her face.

He smiled. "Yes. Yes. Fine. I was just remembering when Jake and Robert brought similar crafts home from school." It was things like this, thought Bud, drifting in and out of conversations that alarms them that I might have another, more serious stroke; that's why they want me to live here. But a person who lives seventy-seven years has a lot of memories. Some you go to in your mind; some Bud knew, come to you.

"Well, let's show you to your room," Helen said. The room was not far. His family had given him the main master bedroom on the first floor, surely, so he would not have to walk up and down the stairs. They must have had to move all their stuff upstairs, Bud thought. All this trouble for me and I haven't even decided how long I'm staying.

The room was big but simple. There was a queen-sized bed with a nightstand on one side that held a lamp. There was a dresser with a mirror on one wall and opposite the bed was what looked like another dresser to Bud, but this one had a twenty-inch television on it. The smell of fresh paint was in the air and the wall color was off-white. Jake made two trips bringing in Bud's three pieces of luggage. He set all of them next to each other on the floor near the foot of the bed. "Thank you, Jake," Bud replied. He turned to Helen, "And thank you for the lovely room." He leaned to her and gave her a kiss on the cheek.

The moment was quickly broken with the slam of a door; someone was home and went through the front door in a hurry. Ah, yes, the teen, thought Bud.

"Is that you Kevin?!" Helen called out.

"Yes. I'm home, Mom!"

Helen looked at her watch but said nothing. She looked up at Bud. "So, do you like the room?" Her eyes were bright, filled with pride. Yes, Bud knew that she sincerely wanted him here as much as anyone. Bud recognized immediately it was not pride in the decoration of the room this woman enjoyed; she took pride in her family and it was obvious that her love knew no depths and her welcome to stay no time limit.

***

As alive as the house was on the day Bud arrived, the day before Thanksgiving found Bud quite alone in the large suburban home. Apparently the kids, with no school this day, each had plans with friends. Jake said with it so close to the end of the month he had to go into the office to *take care of loose ends* as he put it. Helen was doing some last minute grocery shopping; both Jake and Helen had asked Jake to join each of them but he refused, saying that he didn't want to slow either of them down or be in the way.

Bud slept well his first night in the strange place. No doubt he was worn-out from the trip the day before; it had, after all, been a long day. He went for a walk in the morning around the neighborhood and found that the hills had tired him out considerably. When he got back to the house he fixed himself some lunch and took his medication. The joints in his knees ached and he quickly found himself on the couch in front of the television watching an old western on one of the cable stations. It wasn't long before the old man drifted into an early afternoon nap.

Bud wasn't roused from his sleep for nearly three hours when Helen came home from shopping. Bud, at first, was rattled – waking up in a strange place. But there was more. A sense of foreboding swirled through his head. The feeling was strong, one of great sadness but there was no logic to connect it with. Possibly the medication, he thought. As Helen unpacked groceries, Bud lay still on the couch, as if still asleep. He slowly and out of Helen's sight raised a hand to his face; his eyes were damp from tears. A dream, he thought; but certainly a dream that would make me feel so… sad I would remember but he didn't. His mind only gave up one clue: His great-grandson, Kevin.

***

For Bud, the dinner before Thanksgiving was a feast in itself. Helen had made a roast and there were plenty of side dishes to go around. Bud and Jake sat at the ends of the table while Helen sat next to Jake, and Kevin sat to the left of Bud. The twins each sat to Bud's right. Bud could smell some food for tomorrow's meal all ready cooking in the kitchen.

It was then that the young teen, Kevin, turned to his great-grandfather and asked with a mouth full of food, "You were in World War II, right Grampa?"

Bud put down his utensils, swallowed his food and looked at the boy. My God he doesn't look any younger than some of the boys I saw in the Pacific. Bud's body shivered and he hoped no one at the table saw it. Kevin reminded him of someone but could not remember whom. The feeling he had after waking from his nap – that sadness – whirled through him again. He brushed the feeling aside and instead he answered the question, "Yup, I was a marine."

Kevin, still chewing his food asked, "So you weren't at Normandy or Europe or anything like that, huh?"

"No," replied Bud, "I fought the Japanese."

Quickly, the boy responded with enthusiasm, "Were you one of the guys that raised the flag, you know, that famous flag?"

Being a History teacher for so long, Bud almost lashed out at his great-grandson as if he was facing a student that had failed to read the assigned material; nevertheless he kept his composure. But before he could respond, Helen did, "*That* flag raising was on Iwo Jima, on Mount Sarabuchi, right Grampa?" she smiled at the old teacher.

Bud returned the smile, nodded, as he wiped his mouth with his cloth napkin and said, "That is right, my dear, you get an A."

Jake's cell phone rang and he dismissed himself from the table in a hurry. Kevin on the other hand continued with his questioning, "Grampa have you watched *Band of*

Brothers or *Saving Private Ryan* – did you jump out of airplanes?"

Bud shook his head. "No I haven't seen any of those movies and no jumping out of airplanes."

"But you landed on beaches, right?" Kevin continued.

Helen jumped back into the conversation. Jake was off somewhere on his cell phone. "Your Grampa served at a lot of places but mainly Okinawa." She looked at Bud for confirmation even though she knew she was right. But Bud had slipped away again, in his mind, slipped away to another time and another place.

"We haven't studied Okinawa, yet," said Kevin. "That was right before the A-bomb right, Gramps?"

Bud heard the words of his great-grandson; they seemed to echo within his mind. That is the thing with memories, Bud knew, they can hide sometimes for years, generations, then in an instant half a century can become yesterday and last week ages ago. Okinawa. Here on the eve of a Thanksgiving in a new millennium Okinawa was more vivid than anything. Bud was aware of his family around him and he acknowledged that by saying to his great-grandson in a dry voice, "The war in Europe was over before Okinawa started. But just because the Germans had quit did not mean the Japanese had any intentions, son. And, no one, at least guys on Okinawa knew nothing about no Atomic bomb." His grammar had seemed to split back to when he was a young man. He wanted to continue the rest of the story but instead he went back to his meal noticing that almost everyone else at the table was finishing their food. The old man's mind kept him silent company as he ate.

In his mind, Bud heard the guns of all the American warships surrounding Okinawa firing. They were celebrating VE day – victory over Germany; it was May 8th, 1945. "War's over in Europe," one of the leathernecks said.

A somber, young kid said, "I wish it was over here." That was the kid that Kevin reminded Bud of. *That* kid.

Bud shooed the thought from his mind – the thought of that kid. His mind was entrenched in 1945; the fact of the matter was, that while American forces chased women in Berlin and got drunk of off Hitler's champagne in his personal resort, and folks back home in the US celebrated as well, the 6th Marine Division had a job to do; they still had a war to fight. They had to help take Okinawa.

Helen began clearing the table. If she said something to Bud, he did not hear it.

Okinawa was the first island that *was* Japanese territory and the occupants' orders were to defend it to the last man. Indeed, when it was obvious the Americans were going to take the island, the Japanese commander committed ritualistic suicide. By then, Bud was in a hospital in Guam. For the 6th Marine Division in the end there would be one place that would symbolize that island and the battle that was fought there... it was called Sugar Loaf Hill. Nine days of fighting, 7,574 Marines wounded – and people on the other side of the world were celebrating.

Supper was finished.

As they finished clearing the table, Bud, the ex-teacher asked Kevin what he was learning now in History class. "Mainly, current events," the boy replied. "We're studying those wackos in the Middle East that blow themselves up. Absolutely nuts."

"They had kamikazes in the Pacific that did the same thing," Bud said.

"Yeah, but to strap a bomb to *yourself and then blow it up*?!"

Ah, yes, Bud thought, I have been down this path before. History has somewhat glorified those men that flew their planes into American ships as misguided and brainwashed fools but they tend to leave out the rest of the suicidal tactics of the Japanese. Bud taught during the Cold War and the curriculum was slighted for that era. No one wanted to talk about men or women, or children even, strapping satchel explosives to their bodies and throwing themselves under tanks in a war that was over. It was all about the failings and criminality of communism. And now today, no one understands the fanaticism of those homicidal bombers, just like in the sixties when Bud had argued with his son, Robert, about America using the Atomic bomb on civilians to end World War II.

Bud must have whispered the word, *Kyushu*, because Kevin asked what he said. "Nothing," Bud replied. "I am very tired and I haven't unpacked yet. I had all day and I unpacked hardly a thing. I took a nice walk and then had a nice nap, though. The couch is quite comfortable. Helen, thank you for a lovely meal and I look forward to tomorrow, but this old man is worn out."

There were some protests but everyone in the family seemed to have something else they could do. Bud passed hugs and kisses to everyone and thanked them again for the invitation and the accommodations. "You are going to stay through Christmas, Grampa, right?" asked Ursy.

Bud smiled, "You want me to stay and help Santa bring more presents! Is that it?" He tickled her belly making her giggle.

"No," she said. "We want our Grampa here. I'll share the candy from my Christmas stocking with you." Then Ursy turned to her mom, "We can give Grampa his own stocking, right?" Helen of course agreed. "Yeah, you see," said Ursy, "and we get Hershey Kisses and gum drops and Jolly Ranchers..."

"Oh, you'll give me diabetes," laughed Bud. He said one final goodnight and then headed again to a foreign bedroom tucked in welcoming surroundings... He feared he would get little sleep this night since he slept so well the night before and had taken a long nap in the afternoon. But then again, he was an old man.

The bed was quite comfortable, actually, but the shadows on the wall and the placement of the furniture added to the fact that it just wasn't home. The night before he fell right to sleep from exhaustion.

This night, however, while some of the family was still up and moving about the house, Bud actually found some peaceful sleep. But when the house grew quiet Bud jerked awake as if nudged. For a moment he was lost, unsure of where he was then he could sense the smell of fresh paint, which reminded him of his place. And even though he was an old man and had lived through many things, he pulled the covers up close to his chin.

His mind was fully awake now but for a while his mind fixed on no specific subject – he simply felt strange sleeping in an unfamiliar place. Then his mind began replaying the events from earlier in the day – which at this hour meant he was actually thinking about the events of yesterday. It was after midnight; it was officially Thanksgiving Day but sunrise was hours away.

His knees still ached from sitting in coach on the plane ride two days before and his walk from earlier that day. He thought back to his flight. There had been a priest on the plane that made Bud feel the plane was somehow in good hands even though the old man knew the sand in his hourglass was almost completely at the bottom. Bud knew he could go any day now... just like he did when he served in the Pacific... like when he assaulted Sugar Loaf Hill.

Now the ghosts came alive like actors in a play. But no production on stage or film could capture the realism, the horror... the hell – the experience that he kept with him and away from his family his whole life. There was a cast of characters. Poker buddies, friends, replacements that didn't last a day, officers, even the enemy but the stage light cut through the dust in the memories of the old man's mind and cast it's light on one soldier. It was the night before Bud got injured and there in a hole a kid was celebrating his nineteenth birthday crying in his helmet. He cried all night because he knew he was going to die the next day – at least that's what he said. He would say that and ask why the war wasn't over for them? Over and over, all night the kid kept on. It was a damn good question. How the moon and stars can shine on one half of the world celebrating while boys died and celebrated their birthdays in mud filled holes waiting for *their* time to come all too soon?

Bud reached aimlessly for the light on the nightstand next to the bed, almost knocking it over before turning it on. The light chased the demons away for a moment. The old man got up and shuffled under swollen knees to his suitcases that he still had lined at the foot of the bed.

Like a child he knelt, knew exactly which bag to open, which pocket to unzip, exactly where to reach. He found the box and retrieved it. Bud held it in his shaking hand for a long moment before lifting the lid revealing the Purple Heart medal. Bud held the box in his left hand and ran the crooked index finger of his right hand up an down the medal. Strange, he thought, Kevin never asked if I received any medals.

The Purple Heart to Bud was the most honorable of all awards given by the American government, even though it was given out the most. Because unlike other medals, even those that honor bravery, the Purple Heart honors sacrifice, it means you were injured in combat. Bud got his for assaulting Sugar Loaf Hill. The nineteen-year-old kid that cried the whole night before earned his the same day as Bud, although he received it posthumously and it was given to his family. The kid's premonition was right. He died the day after his nineteenth birthday, while the other half of the world celebrated. Bud shuttered to think how other guys that turned nineteen on that same night as that kid celebrated. He simply shuttered. The thoughts of candles and cakes and kisses and liquor and broads disgusted him to this day.

Bud gently closed the lid holding the Purple Heart and lifted himself up. He didn't let the fact that he was up pass by and he used the restroom before returning to bed. He left the light on the nightstand on for some time, trying to focus on good thoughts – thoughts with his wife, his family; then he scolded himself for being afraid of the dark and turned the light out.

He drifted half asleep and when he did the demons wasted no time returning, whispering in his ear. This time they spoke of candy, masquerading their true sinister nature. Floating somewhere between sleep and consciousness he heard his great-grandchildren – the twins – talking about all the Christmas candy they would get. Their innocent voices repeated themselves in Bud's mind; then, they began to distort, their accent changing. Bud felt cold under the covers the bed. He heard the new words now, spoken in broken English coming from a radio.

In his mind, it was 1945 again. His vision was dark and empty, which made the sounds in Bud's mind clearer. It was Japanese propaganda about Okinawa. The voice was of a woman, but there was a reptilian hiss from the mouth from which the words came. In Bud's mind they sounded more baleful then when he first heard them injured as a young man...

Sugar Loaf Hill . . . Chocolate Drop . . . Strawberry Hill. Gee, those places sound wonderful! You can just see the candy houses with the white picket fences around them and the candy canes hanging from the trees, their red and white stripes glistening in the sun. But the only thing red about those places is the blood of Americans. Yes, sir, those are the names of hills in southern Okinawa where the fighting's so close that you get down to bayonets and sometimes your bare fists. Artillery and naval gunfire are all right when the enemy is far off but they don't do you any good when he's right in the same foxhole with you. I guess it's natural to idealize the worst places with pretty names to make them seem less awful. Why Sugar Loaf has changed hands so often it looks like Dante's Inferno. Yes, sir, Sugar Loaf Hill . . . Chocolate Drop . . . Strawberry Hill. They sound good, don't they? Only those who've been there know what they're really like.

Bud was recovering in Guam when he heard the Japanese broadcast – he and other Marines wounded trying to take Sugar Loaf Hill. The men had taken to listening to some Japanese broadcasts because they sometimes played good Big Band music. It was an attempt by the enemy to make the soldiers homesick. It didn't work, because you were always homesick so you didn't need any music or propaganda to make you miss it more but *that* broadcast hit too close to home for those recovering from their wounds. Bud, like other soldiers there were injured early in the assault of Sugar Loaf Hill. Each of them knew that more were sent; more were injured, maimed or killed. It was the worse casualties Bud's 6th Marine Division took in the war.

Dreams and nightmares follow no script. Bud's were no different. In his mind he found himself back on the airliner that brought him to Atlanta. The plane was disproportioned and a nurse was serving drinks. But the priest was still in his seat. Stoic. Just as he had been during the real flight.

Suddenly the plane hit rough turbulence and it rolled hard to the right. There were screams… and then small arms fire? Nambu gunfire – Japanese machine gunfire! Orders being called out. Screams for Corpsmen. Bud could still see the priest… except he was no longer a priest and they were no longer on the plane.

The man now was a chaplain leaning over a fallen Marine in the mud of Okinawa. Bud was remembering an actual event. Before Bud had been evacuated he witnessed this scene that was now being played for Bud like an old movie reel through a rusty projector in Bud's mind.

Bud watched now in his sleep like he did on that day on Okinawa. Both the chaplain and the wounded soldier had blond hair, except the wounded soldier's was brushed with blood. The two men whispered between each other and held hands. Gripping one another with knowing anguish that soon their grip would not be felt by one. They seemed to Bud, to comfort each other, an odd thing Bud thought. A dying man consoling a chaplain. Then it happened; the injured Marine could no longer squeeze back. The hunched chaplain turned to Bud who was only ten feet away. "At least he died with family," said the chaplain. He must have seen a puzzled look on Bud's face. "He's my brother," the chaplain said, his voice shaken but not broken. There were tears, but this chaplain had lain to rest many a Marine and in the end his brother was no different then the ones that had fallen before him – except he died in the arms of family.

Bud jerked awake. He lifted a hand to his face. His cheeks were wet. Dawn was rising and the shadows in his room were gray. Bud checked the clock on the nightstand; morning was indeed here. He stretched. The house was silent. It was peaceful. It was full of people, family – Bud's family, and it was peaceful.

It was before Thanksgiving dinner that Bud was given the honor of saying grace. The family held hands in a circle around the table. Bud had Kevin in his left hand and Jake on his right. Four generations of male Velniks were chained together by their hands.

Bud had nothing prepared to say; in fact, his first few words were probably repeated around the country a million times over. How many Thanksgivings had Bud celebrated since it was celebrated? How many prayers had he said or heard? He spoke as he thought, repeating what he had heard over the years; then he thought of that dying Marine clutching the hands of his brother, the chaplain. He thought of the chaplain's words and Bud Velznik finished his prayer at Sugar Loaf with, "I give thanks to God for allowing me to hold the hands of my family all full with life and love and peace. And those separated from their love ones on this day – even on the other side of the world – *you* are at least in *my* heart and prayers. Amen."

Lot 1412

Deputy Thomas Sabel could see the lights of the city from here and the tops of the tallest buildings. He could see them only for a moment as he drove past through an opening of trees. Out here there were still pastures with cows and horses. The sprawl of the city had not reached out to these rural surroundings yet. Night was just now claiming the sky and Sabel was just beginning his shift.

The road was lumped with hills and every chance he got Deputy Sabel would try to catch a glimpse of the city lights or buildings off in the distance as he drove his cruiser to his designated area of patrol. As an officer of a rural county with limited funds, Sabel's usual patrol was the whole county but this county was fast becoming a suburb; in fact, it was one of the fastest growing counties in the nation. With growth came money and business and homes... and crime. Tonight, Deputy Sabel's orders came direct from the sheriff. Sabel was to patrol a newly developing neighborhood where builders had recently brought complaints of vandalism to the sheriff.

Vandalism, thought Sabel, is the crime he investigates and, yet, Susan thinks he could still get shot here

– here in this small shadow of the big city. Susan and Tom, as he was called, were high school sweethearts that grew up in a neighborhood, which at that time was considered a quaint and upscale suburb – middleclass. Now, that neighborhood and area was sprawl, part of the lights of the city that darted through the trees that Deputy Sabel now passed. It'll happen here, thought Sabel, everything will spread to even here – the congestion, the density, the noise. It was all ready happening, really; when Sabel went to get a haircut he would overhear the barbers talking about how they remember nothing but dirt roads and street signs instead of paved, congested streets and traffic lights. That was ten short years ago.

The couple, Susan and Tom, recently moved in together about two years ago but neither Susan nor Tom's parents knew the arrangement. Each set of parents had moved from where they had raised their children. About the same time Tom and Susan thought it practical to move in together – out in what was called the *Outskirt suburbs* by many locals. However, they were living a lie to each of their parents by living together – and a tough one at that. Susan had kept a charade that she lived with a girlfriend. That charade was put to the test last Labor Day when Susan's parents came to spend the weekend. Susan's friend, Kim, was at the beach that weekend with her boyfriend. Still, the highly pious parents kept pointing out that it would be much more practical, as well as righteous, if Tom would just propose.

Tom was now turning into the subdivision and away from the lights of the city. The brick signs that were to welcome people to the neighborhood looked freshly completed and well lit. All kinds of shrubs and flowers adorned the new signs that read, *Kindred Acres*. Not very original, thought Sabel but then again they were being built by Kindred Homes, Incorporated, one of the best names in home building around these parts. And if you didn't know it, there was another sign that read told you, *Kindred Homes –*

We don't just don't make houses, we make homes... starting in the low $300,000s. That was too rich for Deputy Sabel's blood but maybe his soul might cover it; and Susan's income from being the receptionist at the Cadillac dealership didn't help. Sure when she finished getting her doctorate things would be better, but for now... now things were tight.

Below the Kindred sign there was another smaller sign, the words painted in black on a piece of useless plywood. This sign read, *Hablamos Espanol.* "We speak Spanish," Sabel said to himself. That is probably why Sam Kindred himself waited to come into today to tell the sheriff, not only about more vandalism, but of the... well, obvious signs that someone or some people had been eating, sleeping and relieving themselves overnight in various empty houses – all ways a different house; and the night-tenant was all ways gone before any worker got there by sunrise. There were traces of some fast food wrappers, porno magazines, and lots and lots of empty liquor bottles, of all varieties and price ranges including a bottle of very expensive scotch. All this could be attributed to teenagers – just as the vandalism – had it not been for the events that happened two nights before. But Kindred also waited because he knew most of the workers that built his houses were illegal immigrants and he didn't want any heat coming down on him about that.

For two weeks there had been break-ins in neighborhoods surrounding and not far from Kindred Acres. The break-ins, although not humorous, were odd. It seemed that the perpetrator would force his or her entry into a house, take things that he or she thought to be valuable and if there was a purse or wallet around take any cash. That, however, was not the odd thing. The odd thing was that the perp would take as much hard liquor as he could carry. So when the crimes were first being committed, the police officers thought it was a gang of teenagers or a petty thief. Then, one week ago there was another break-in that fit the profile of the others except this time a gun was stolen – a .45 caliber Glock to be precise – similar to the one Deputy Sabel was now carrying. In addition, a World War II veteran that was visiting relatives was shot and killed when the robber took the gun. The old man must have surprised the guy and took a bullet for it.

When Deputy Sabel went into Sheriff Montrose's office before his shift tonight Sabel noticed a slender man, his face deep in thought, wringing the brim of a baseball cap leaving the sheriff's office. Sabel later learned from the sheriff that the man was Sam Kindred himself. Apparently, beyond the vandalism, there was something else going on at Kindred Acres.

The police had a lot of leads but the best one they got just might have been the one Sam Kindred gave today.

At about the same time the break-ins were occurring was about the same time workers began noticing that someone was sleeping in some of the unfinished homes. If it was the same person, then that person had been using an unlived in Kindred home as his hideout. Everyone knew about the vandalism. Hell, last weekend a couple of teenagers destroyed the inside of one house the night before the homeowners were to move in by having a paintball fight in the house. It sure as hell made a mess and the kids left some empty beer cans, but on the same night, at a different house in the subdivision, someone else had broke in and spent the night with a few bottles of booze.

Kindred had a delusion of grandeur for the subdivision; Sabel could tell that as he kept driving through the winding, newly paved streets. Man, thought Sabel, old Kindred sure did cut down some trees to make room for these lots and houses. The houses were almost stacked one on top of the other. And the ones that were built were huge.

Some of the homes all ready had residents and for those houses there were little signs staked in the growing grass of the front yard that read *Private Residence*. Some driveways had cars parked; some homes had lights on and in most Deputy Sabel could see the flickering colors of a television set on inside.

Some homes were nothing but graded lots; some homes were merely A-frames and others were almost completed. Few had trees in the yards, Sabel noticed. Sabel passed the little mobile home that acted as the builder's office and several portable toilets. It was while he was slowly moving around a curve he saw the parked car. And everything changed from there.

The car was a luxury sedan. It was one of those nice Mercedes E-class sedans. It was parked on the curb, facing the same direction that Sabel was traveling but the car was against the curb on the opposite lane. Sabel slowed and pulled in behind the car.

He did not flash his dome lights; the car was parked in front of a finished home and it could be a realtor making sure everything was all right, or an anxious owner taking one more look at the house before they moved in. After all, the night was still young. Despite that, Deputy Sabel called Dispatch and ran the plates to make sure the car was not stolen.

It wasn't. It belonged to a guy named Xavier Ralston. Well, thought, Sabel that better be who's behind the wheel… or his wife. With his headlights on, Sabel could only see one person in the car; he flashed his dome lights just so the person in the car would not get antsy about a car pulling up behind them and let them know it was the police. Then, Deputy Thomas Sabel radioed Dispatch one more time about investigating the car and exited his cruiser with the engine still running.

Sabel had only been an officer three years now but some things were instinctive, like pulling his Mag-Lite flashlight from his belt and turning it on. There were no streetlights so the area was lit only by the lights from the officer's car and the air smelled of tilled dirt and fresh lumber. His right hand slid down to his holster and his fingertips touched the grip of his gun.

As Sabel cautiously approached the car, he shined his flashlight in the vehicle. The driver side window slid down; Sabel let it come all the way down. He was at the back of the car now and saw no movement, no one in the backseat. "Keep your hands on the steering wheel, please!" He called out to the driver.

Sabel was at the backseat window of the car; he shined his light on the driver and saw both hands gripped around the steering wheel. They were the hands of a white male. There was no one in the passenger seat; that seat was filled with papers and folders and Sabel thought he saw a box on the floorboard. But Sabel heard something... something coming from inside the car.

He leaned towards the driver side window and flashed his light inside the car and looked. A well-dressed man in a blue pinstripe suit with a red tie sat in the driver's seat. He's a realtor, thought, Sabel. Then the man turned to him. His face was overall ashen but his cheeks and eyes were red and blotchy. The man was sobbing and his tears shined on his cheeks and swollen eyes.

The man quickly turned away, the light obviously hurt his eyes.

Deputy Thomas Sabel was stunned. He removed the flashlight from the man's face and pointed it towards the ground. "Is something the matter, sir?" asked Sabel. "Are you injured?"

The well-dressed man gave a chuckle that made mucous run from his nose; tears dripped from his face into his lap. The man took a handkerchief from the breast pocket of his suit and wiped his face. He chuckled once more then shook his head. Sable was confused, "Sir, are you all right? Are you in any danger?" Sable lifted his head up for a moment to see if there was anyone lurking around that he missed. He scanned the area with his flashlight but only for a moment before returning his attention to the man in the car.

The man, still shaking his head must have realized how the situation looked and turned to the officer and forced a smile veiled by tears. "No officer, I'm not injured," he chuckled, "at least not physically." He leaned forward towards the steering wheel and looked passed Deputy Sabel. "That was to be our home," the man said, almost breaking down into tears.

Sabel looked over his left shoulder at the completed all brick house. Sabel could tell the sod had just been laid and there was a sapling of some kind in the middle of the yard, held up by three guide wires. A flowerbed lined the walkway up to the door. It was a nice house, one that he hoped he and Susan might have one day. He turned his attention back to the man in the car. "I don't understand," said Sable.

"No," said the man. "Well, officer, to make a long story short my fiancée broke up with me today. This was to be our house – our home – where we raised our children," he began to sob again, "and have a family," he said.

"Maybe she just got cold feet…"

"No, no, no," the man insisted. "She has been hesitant through everything." He rubbed his face with his handkerchief again. "Funny, it's all ways the woman that goes overboard with everything – the wedding, the house, all that. But Susan wasn't ready for it; it was all moving too fast for her." The man paused for a moment. "Are you married, officer?"

"No," Sabel said but he didn't want to tell this poor man that he was living with a woman that had the same name as his ex.

The man nodded then looked passed Deputy Sabel, back at the house, all the while nodding. "I looked forward to coming home and being greeted with laughing children and a smiling wife and home cooked meals and holidays with a large family. Even now I can see the children that will never be running through the sprinkler in the yard, learning to ride a bike in the driveway as I delicately hold on to the seat..." The man in the luxury sedan could go on no more; he had broke down and was weeping like a mother at a child's funeral.

Sabel looked into the passenger seat, full of papers, folders, boxes and the one shoebox on the floorboard of the car. Sabel wanted to console the man but he had to make his rounds. "Are you going to be all right?" the deputy asked. "You... you promise me you aren't gonna hurt yourself are you?" Sabel realized he never even asked for the man's driver's license. "By the way, I didn't get your name," Sabel said.

"Xavier Ralston," the man replied, "here's my license. I took it out when you pulled up." Deputy Sabel flashed his light on it; the smiling man on the photo matched the face of the man crying in the car.

"Thank you, Xavier, I've got to make my rounds but if you're still here I'll check on you. If you're gone, I wish you all the best Mr. Ralston." Sabel didn't even wait for a reply; he just headed back to his idling cruiser. The whole walk back he looked at the house. He could imagine everything Xavier imagined and it made his heart ache. He wished he could give his Susan a home as nice as the one he was staring at. Before he got back in his police car he noticed the sales sign in the front yard. There was an *Under Contract* sign lining the top of it. That will probably be down by this time tomorrow, Sabel thought. Then there was a second sign right at the curb that had all the zoning and building information. This house was built on Lot 1412.

Back in his cruiser, Deputy Sabel radioed Dispatch and explained that it was just a homeowner checking on the progress of his new home. He pulled his cruiser around Xavier Ralston's Mercedes and started patrolling the rest of the winding streets of Kindred Acres. Yes, this would be a nice place to raise a family. Man, this was a *huge* neighborhood. Lot 1412. Sabel wondered if there were over fifteen hundred lots in this place. The more he drove and saw the completed homes the more he fell in love with the area. Even the partially built homes were engaging. A neighborhood like this needs a guardhouse and a wall around it to keep out the vandals and the liquor stealing creeps, Sabel thought. His mind snapped back to attention. He was after all on duty.

That's when Deputy Thomas Sabel's life changed.

His car was cresting a street high on a hill. Down to his left, he looked down on what was supposed to be Xavier Ralston's home. Sabel could still see Ralston's car parked at the curb. Suddenly, inside Ralston's car, Deputy Thomas Sabel saw a flash of light followed by what sounded like a firecracker... or a gun. At the same time, something had jumped in front of his cruiser. It was a figure of a person in a long coat holding what looked to be a long barreled pistol. Sabel hit the brakes and ducked at the same time. He heard what sounded like rubber pellets thumping his cruiser by the dozens.

After only a few seconds the barrage stopped and the deputy heard laughter. He sat up in his car; his heart racing but he could not see a thing. His windshield and windows were covered in yellow paint. Damn kids! He knew there was more than one because he was hit on all sides of the car and he heard more than one person laughing. Meanwhile, Ralston, what happened to Xavier Ralston?

Sabel rolled down his window and stuck his head out to see. At the same time he ran his windshield wipers with the spray going. He turned around in a driveway and hit his dome lights. For some reason, he did not turn on his siren or call Dispatch.

As his cruiser pulled up in front of Xavier Ralston's car, Deputy Sabel's headlights were shining into the darkness of Ralston's quiet Mercedes. Sabel hit his high beams. Blood. There was blood on the windshield. Sabel called Dispatch for backup.

Sabel was out of his paint soaked car and ran to the passenger side of the car since it was the closest. He pulled the door handle and the door swung open. Inside, Xavier Ralston lay in a pool of blood, slumped over in the passenger seat.

Sabel quickly retrieved his Mag Lite flashlight and surveyed the scene. He saw the bullet hole in the left side of Mr. Ralston's head. In his lap lay a revolver with his left hand on it. Sabel saw the man was dead, clearly. The gun was not the same as the one reported stolen that killed the Marine. It appeared to Sabel that some of those folders contained documents for the house and others contained love letters, birthday and Valentine cards. Then there on the floorboard of the passenger side something sparkled bright when the light from his flashlight hit it.

With sirens wailing in the background, Deputy Sabel leaned down and there among the old love letters and almost untouched by blood was a brilliant piece of jewelry. It was an engagement ring – and an expensive one at that. The diamond and the cut and the setting were just like the ones Susan all ways circled in magazines or stopped in the mall jewelry stores to look at.

With his left hand, Deputy picked the ring off the floorboard. It sparkled under the light of his flashlight. The ring had been lying by itself on the floorboard. All the boxes, folders and papers were now in the passenger seat with Xavier Ralston's body slumped over them. A suicide note, thought Sabel. There could be a suicide note wanting his fiancée to have the ring.

He searched the blood-soaked car with his flashlight, still clutching the ring in his left hand. He saw nothing. The sirens were growing closer; he looked at the ring once more under his Mag-Lite. The ring was beautiful and there was an inscription on the inside of the band. It read, *For my love, Susan, my only love.*

Deputy Thomas Sabel stood now. He looked at the house built on Lot 1412. He could see himself on one knee proposing and he could see coming home and being greeted with laughing children and a smiling wife and home cooked meals and holidays with a large family. He could see children running through the sprinkler in the yard, learning to ride a bike in the driveway as Sabel delicately steadied the bike by the seat.

"I hope there is not a suicide note," he said to himself and slipped the ring into his front pocket. It was dark now and he could hear the other police cruisers arriving. It was a dark evening with no moon; Deputy Thomas Sabel could see the lights of the city in the distance. Like the barbers feared it would spread, the sprawl would eventually spread out to here.

The deputy then looked at his cruiser. It was covered in paint from pranksters. It will wash off he thought. He was now bathed in the lights the cars of his fellow officers.

And Susan thought I would get shot out here.

Lullaby

People said when Teddy Roosevelt died in his sleep that it was the only way he would go, else Death would get a fight.

Death must have agreed to the terms. No matter. But did Teddy fight? Hmm, I know the answer but I will only whisper it to *you* when you are safe in your bed…

And any evening I choose…

Are you awake?

Of course you are. Well, let us simply say that you are aware of me. That is good enough and all that really matters.

What's that? Am I Death? What does it matter to you? Oh, I guess it matters a lot but would you rather I be a bullet, a car wreck, a plane crash, a fire? No this is what you want. *This* is what *you* want. This is what *everyone* wants… and I find it… charming.

Lullaby. Shall I sing? *Go to sleep…*

No. Let us get on with this.

You are dying in your sleep. My voice may be real or may be just your brain misfiring, having its death throe. Try to move. Do you feel the pain in your chest, your brain? Oh, you can't move and here you are trying to scream.

Tell me...

What is going through your mind right now? Are there children, perhaps down the hallway even? Is there a warm body slowly sleeping next to you that you can't rustle awake? Ha! Or are you sadly alone? Do you even know, now? I know like Teddy and everyone else there are deeds, ah yes, deeds undone. You thought you had more time. Tsk. Tsk. Yup, everyone always thinks they do.

You know it is believed that some welcome me. But no one really does no matter their situation.

Shall I console? Shall I, as your dying body doesn't move. Yet you thrash and thrash and thrash in a sack that can no longer budge.

Here is comfort: People will say that you went in your sleep! *That is the way to go!* Ha ha! They will say you look more peaceful; that you are at peace and there is no more pain and that you didn't... suffer...

But...

You and I know different.

They will even say you are in a better place now...

Is there?

That is for me to know... and for you to soon find out. What do you believe? Whatever it is are you ready for it? Were you ready for this?

No. No. There is no bargaining.

Come along now.

Go to sleep... Go to sleep... Lullaby...

Sharks and Minnows

The Fourth of July was still a week away but summer vacation was in full swing for Becky Garrett and the other children at the Eves Glen Recreational Center. Even at midmorning the pool was bustling. Most of the children were in the water; those that weren't were hurrying to and from the bathrooms or lounging about near the shady concession area.

It was from within the maintenance room that the heart of the pool whined, recycling and filtering the water and pumping it back into the pool. Only the maintenance people had access to the machinery, and most swimmers hardly heard or paid notice to the constant, mechanical hum.

The concession area was a nice gathering place, complete with a snack bar that served chips, candy bars, ice cream sandwiches and hot dogs. Wooden picnic tables, shaded from the sun by a covered roof, offered people not only a place to eat and chat but also shelter from the seething sun or the occasional thunderstorm or shower.

Away from the shade of the concession area the pool and surrounding area was active with frenetic life. The sound of splashing water, giggling and screaming children was constant, as was the shouts from mothers to their kids running too fast or splashing water in their sibling's faces. Music and disc jockeys from different radio stations played inharmoniously in the air. On occasion, the whistle of a watchful lifeguard, perched upon a ten-foot chair overlooking the playful madness, broke all sounds.

The smell of chlorine and tanning oil filled the air. Anxious children fidgeted as mothers tried to apply suntan lotion to soft and pale skin. Only traces of white, feathery clouds brushed the blue summer sky. The sun's rays beat down unabated – much to the delight of Becky and the other children. Indeed, Eves Glen Recreational Center was open for business – its twentieth summer.

Facing away from the concession stand, steps on each corner of the pool led swimmers who liked to ease themselves into the water entry to the shallow end of the pool, which had a meager depth of three feet. Like most pools, the further a person walked from the stairs in the shallow end the deeper the water became. It was an olympic-size pool for the long part of the L-shape; the deep end made-up the short part of the L-shape and it was roped off from the shallow end. Two diving boards, a low one and a high one, graced the deep end. At its deepest, the pool was twelve feet from the surface to the bottom. When the diving boards were closed on every even hour of the day, as they were now, children usually played Sharks and Minnows in the deep end.

Becky was one of them.

Being twelve meant that Becky Garrett did not need to be accompanied by an adult. She merely had to bring her pool pass to gain entrance. The previous year, when Becky's cousin visited, both girls had to be accompanied by either girl's mother. The two girls shared the same birthday, January twenty-seventh; only Becky was exactly one year older. At times, last summer, it had been an inconvenience on both child and adult to get to the pool as often as the girls wanted to; the adults had their agenda and the girls had theirs – the pool. But Becky's cousin being there that summer was a relief. Becky's mother and stepfather had separated in May of that year, which made it all the better that Becky's cousin was there. The two girls could play while the two adults could do, well... whatever adults do. Mainly, observed Becky, the two women complained about men and drank wine. After awhile, though, they would stop complaining and start laughing like sisters. And sometimes they cried together, like sisters.

Becky herself was an only child so she enjoyed the company of her cousin. She sometimes wondered what it would be like to have a brother or sister but her mom once explained it was impossible. But Becky was a very outgoing kid. She had many friends and played sports all year round. The sport depended on the season.

The separation between Becky's mom and stepfather put a pall over last summer for sure and Becky found herself drifting, in some ways, apart from her mother. There had already been some small distance between Becky and her stepdad. Even though Becky loved her stepdad, the fact was that Becky never knew her real father. And sometimes, like late at night when Becky was alone with her thoughts, for some reason it made a difference. To Becky, her stepdad had always been her *real* father. She called him Dad and she loved him yet there was always a feeling in Becky that maybe kept her not as close as other kid's were to their parents. She thought about that often, especially now as she reached her teen years, but the main feeling she had – that she kept inside - was a feeling that this man was not the man Becky's mother had, as adult's put it, expressed her love with someone that resulted in the birth of Becky. No *that* man, for reasons unknown to a twelve year old girl, had taken off – saw no need to stick around and be a father. After a summer of Becky's mom belittling her stepdad, the two reconciled before the start of school. Why? Becky was simply told they had "worked things out like grown-ups." For as long as Becky could remember, her mom told her how lucky they were to have him - that all men were not as good as him and they could not survive without him. And Becky did love him; he was a good man with a great sense of humor that cared for her and was at every swim meet and school play, but somewhere deep down she resented the fact that he was *needed*. She accepted what her feelings told her at this age, that boys were desirable and finding a good one may be important in life but *needing* one? Even at her age, she did not like that idea.

But that was last summer and this year was different. Becky could come and go as she pleased – just as long as her mom knew where she was. On this mid-morning summer day she promised her mom that she would be home sometime between one and two o'clock in the afternoon. So Becky had about three hours to spend playing at the pool with her friends. Becky was also coming to that age where she recognized boys and wanted to *be* recognized by boys. She also saw boys as childish and clumsy, self-interested and cruel. They were like puppies, cute in a way but always bouncing around making messes and traveling in packs, concerned with attention from their peers. Only the older high school boys seemed mature, like the ones that were lifeguards at Eves Glen. Still, she preferred that her mother was not present to embarrass her. Being by herself gave her a sense of independence. Something, she realized, she never felt before.

However there was one hitch to her freedom today. Becky had lied to her mother. She had told her that she was going to the pool with her best friend, Ellie, and Ellie's mother. Even though Becky was old enough by Eves Glen's rules to be there unaccompanied by an adult, Becky's mother didn't want Becky going to the pool alone. Becky knew that on the last day of school a month earlier an eleven-year-old girl vanished on her way home from her bus stop. The girl did not go to Becky's school, but it was close enough to concern all the parents. Since it happened, all the kids had overheard the grown-ups whispering about it.

Becky was unconcerned. The girl that was missing was a year younger than her and Becky imagined her to be naïve and frail and gullible. All the things Becky wasn't. If confronted with any danger, Becky knew she would resist, fight and eventually overcome. Besides, summer vacation was not about concerns or homework but of carefree days. And right now she only cared about winning in pool games and showing up the boys.

Becky was physically stronger than most boys her age – and when she got the chance she liked to prove it. The game Sharks and Minnows often gave her that opportunity. She was the top swimmer on the Eves Glen Recreational Center Girls Swim Team – ages eleven - thirteen, of course. The Swimming Apollos they were called. Becky hated the name but since there were boys and girls on the team, the name seemed to cover both sexes. Becky was on the first team of the Apollo swimmers – that meant the best team sponsored by Eves Glen. Their last season, they didn't seem to do so well. In fact, someone made the joke that it was the swim team that never got off the ground. No one found the joke amusing, except maybe the person who made it up and Becky really never got it except that there were some play on words with ground and water or something. *Whatever*, she thought.

Becky was really upset with her team's poor performance because she really enjoyed swimming – and winning. Well, truth be told, she just loved the water. When the pool was not that busy or if she got to the pool early before swim practice, Becky loved to hold her breath underwater and close her eyes and just float weightlessly. She figured that the feeling must be like what astronauts feel in space. It was so peaceful. Becky so enjoyed that peace and so enjoyed the water that gave it to her.

But Sharks and Minnows was organized and run by the boys of the pool, usually between the ages of twelve and thirteen. Sometimes older kids, fourteen or fifteen, would feel a need to impose their will on a game and organize it, which Becky and the younger kids knew meant they were going to be dunked forcibly underwater and held until either they thrashed or the on duty lifeguard blew the whistle or called them by name to cease.

One kid, A.J., was particularly callous. Barely fourteen, he wasn't as tall as the other kids his age; in fact, he was the shortest out of the kids he hung out with. He had fair skin with red hair and his body was covered with freckles. A.J. was the one the younger kids feared most. Becky knew he was particularly mean to the younger boys. She had seen him pull down the swimming trunks of boys waiting in line at one of the diving boards. He would dunk boys and girls alike, splash water in their eyes and smear suntan lotion in their hair. He would check the skimmer for dead toads or crickets and if found he pulled them out; he liked to put them on girls' shoulders or drop them down a boys swim trunks. He was even known to have done a can-opener from the high-dive towards the side of the pool, sending a splash that drenched a woman that was lounging in a chair reading a hardback book and not dressed for swimming. Of course, during such antics, A.J. always broke the surface fighting back a grin and acting as if it was a terrible mistake.

Worse, boys would stay out of the restroom when A.J. was around, which Becky was sure, led to more warm, pee spots in the pool from boys too scared to get out. There had been rumors of A.J. and some other kids stealing the trunks from a kid then sneaking out of the restroom and throwing the trunks in the big trashcan next to the concession stand. Becky had talked to some kids and learned that one of A.J.'s favorite gags was to push a boy while he was standing, helplessly, peeing at a urinal. Apparently, Becky learned, there were stand-up peeing urinals at different heights, one for kids and another for grown-ups. If a young or short kid were standing at the adult one when A.J. pushed him he would have to regain his balance by putting his hand in the urinal.

The girls had their own bullies but none were present this day; Becky was not picked-on often, nor was she intimidated by A.J. or anyone else for that matter, especially in the pool where she felt quite at home. Plus, she was certain the lifeguard would enforce order.

Seventeen-year-old Sarah Harver was the lifeguard on duty. Becky liked her. Sarah helped out on the swim team and she was always very nice to Becky – always smiling. She didn't seem consumed with being a lifeguard like some of the boys – although Becky did like lifeguard, Brett Asa, even though Brett looked down on the younger kids. Shoot, Brett was in high school and had outgrown childish behavior like A.J.'s. But Sarah was friendly and she would not take any garbage from the likes of A.J.

Sarah sat and watched from the umbrella-shaded lifeguard stand in her red one-piece suit like the ones Becky had seen lifeguard's wearing in commercials for the old *Baywatch* show that her stepdad liked to watch. Sarah sat legs crossed, twirling her whistle around her index finger, winding and unwinding it, keeping a keen eye as A.J. organized Sharks and Minnows.

Thirteen kids were playing and A.J. volunteered to be shark first.

Everyone knew the rules; they were simple. The person who was the shark treaded water as the other kids – the minnows – dove from one side of the pool. The shark had to tag someone on the head, not underwater by the way, before that person touched the other side of the pool; if the shark did that then the tagged minnow became a shark on the next round and tried to capture minnows as well. Also, if a shark touched the wall before a minnow jumped, the minnow was a shark. Whether or not the player had left the wall before the shark touched it caused the most arguments. The winner was the player that made it safely across every round and was the last minnow.

During the frenzy of the game it was not uncommon for hair to be pulled, trunks yanked – sometimes completely off – or to be held underwater until gargled screams came from kids that were then allowed to dart to the surface, gasping and clawing; it was then that the shark tagged the kid's head. The only safe place during the game, besides the wall, was twelve feet below the surface where a metal grate covered a drain that sucked water from the bottom of the pool and sent it through the pool's cleaning system.

A.J. was astute to the rules and proficient in the game. He took his place in the pool and was treading water eyeing each of the minnows that were lined and standing on the side of the pool. Like a true predator he searched for the weakest prey. His eyes landed on the kid to Becky's right, an eleven-year-old girl. A.J. smiled a sly grin that reminded Becky of Dr. Seuss's Grinch. A.J. treaded water until he was directly in front of his chosen quarry.

It was instinct that once the shark zeroed-in on one person, the other minnows, not feeling threatened, dove like seals into the water and made a mad dash for safety to the other side. This is what happened. All but four kids went in the first wave. Becky was among those that dove. She reached the other side of the pool before any of the other kids. A.J.'s attention was fixed on the one girl. Becky watched as the poor girl stood on the edge of the pool, her arms crossed and slightly shivering. She grinned an uneasy grin and looked up at the other kids in the game, all treading water and hanging safely to the opposite side of the pool. She looked for help. But what could be done? The girl was doomed.

A.J. inched closer to the wall.

The girl took two strides to her left hoping she could flank past A.J.'s right. To Becky her movements were clumsy and what was a poor attempt at a dive was really a good belly flop that brought laughs from the kids watching. A.J. was to her in seconds. He placed his hand on her head, tagging her; but that wasn't enough, he lifted himself out of the water dunking the poor kid back under. From her seat, the lifeguard Sarah, shouted A.J.'s name and called for him to cut it out. A.J. turned, but did not free the girl as if he didn't hear. Sarah yelled again, causing kids and parents to look. Reluctantly, he relinquished and the girl flailed to the surface coughing.

Becky thought it looked as if A.J. apologized but if he had his face lacked any sincerity. The poor girl rubbed her eyes for a moment then reassured Sarah that she was okay. Sarah reprimanded A.J. once more to keep him in check, to let him know that she was watching him. Becky knew, however, that it made no difference to A.J. He looked at his friends lined up against the wall as the girl continued to cough. His mouth was below the surface hiding his grin; bubbles boiled to the surface. He was laughing.

Becky hated his laugh, especially the way he laughed at the cost of others. She made her decision. She would not fall prey to the likes of A.J. If he singled her out, thought that he would get a laugh at her expense, he was in for a surprise. Becky knew she was a stronger swimmer than A.J. – knew that she could hold her breath longer and if he made a point to embarrass her, she would retaliate. Becky was tired of seeing fear on the faces of other kids while A.J. and his friends gloated. No, she would be ready. And in her mind she pictured grappling around A.J., her arm around his throat preventing him from moving and holding him underwater until he struggled – until he was scared.

She would not get her chance soon. Several rounds went by with A.J. commanding the other sharks where to go and which minnows to go after. During each round, as more sharks hunted, more minnows were caught until only four minnows remained - three of A.J.'s friends and Becky. A grin that was more like a sneer infected A.J.'s freckled face. Becky detested the look. It was full of warped confidence from a boy that was used to getting his way.

He had chosen Becky. Becky knew that to A.J. she would be good quarry; she would struggle and that would make it all the more fun. Ultimately, she was a frail girl that needed to be reminded of it.

As A.J.'s minions treaded towards the wall, the three other boys, friends of A.J.'s, each gave a mocking grin to Becky then dove in the pool and swam to the other side uncontested.

Becky was the one.

She had a plan. She would show A.J. up, beat him physically and mentally and ultimately embarrass him in front of everyone; Becky would wipe that sneer from A.J.'s face.

Without hesitation, Becky made a quick, steep dive avoiding the children's hands that stretched out to touch her head before she hit the water. Many an argument had erupted over the tagging of one's head before it hit the water, but not this time. Becky hit the water and the sounds of the world balked at the surface. The muddled sounds of laughter and splashing were all that existed here; Becky swam straight for the bottom of the pool. She was used to the chlorine by now but her vision was a wavy distortion of shades of blue. Clear and clean. The pressure in her head tightened the deeper she went. Her ears popped and plinked but she was close. There at the bottom, through the swirls of blue was safety in the form of an eighteen by eighteen inch grate that covered the pool's drain. This was the mouth that consumed the water and fed it back through the pipes and into that storage area where only maintenance people went. The pump was locked away in its own room between the bathrooms and the concession stand, always humming its mechanical hum, usually unnoticed, recycling the water and filtering the pee. With Becky's hand on it she could not be tagged. That was the rule. She would stay there at the bottom of the pool and outlast the sharks. She knew she could easily swim to the other side without a breath but she also knew that if she did that A.J. or one of the others would wrap around her like a squid and force her to the surface. This way she would wait until she saw all the legs treading, heads above the water then push safely to the side, skimming the bottom of the pool the whole way. She would outlast them all.

Every spring the pool was drained and cleaned, as Becky knew, and they must have cleaned the drain like Becky's stepdad sometimes did with the shower, with some long snake-like thing. The grate itself was bent and some of the metal bars were cracked and broken. It had its advantages. Becky was able to slip her fingers where the grate was broken to anchor her. Water rushed past her hand into the drain. She expelled air and looked above. All around kids were hovering, arms and legs swirling, cheeks puffed, watching her. In the center was A.J., his red hair gently floating away from his head. He hovered like a jellyfish. Becky almost gave a smile; she wasn't even close to running out of air and if A.J. came, *she* would entangle him until he panicked and squirmed for the surface.

A.J. did expel air and descended towards Becky. The other kids were already pushing for the surface. Some moved towards the pool wall that Becky needed to get to, acting like some sort of blockade. Becky knew A.J.'s intentions; he would try to pull Becky off the grate and then squeeze the air out of her until she quit. If A.J. went to the surface, Becky would push off towards safety. She would outlast him.

A.J. reached for Becky's arm; she pulled away and when she did she pulled the grate covering the drain. Becky was used to the placement of the grate and instead of holding the grate, she instinctively put her right hand where it once was. There was only a hole now. A small manmade mouth that's purpose was to pull water from the pool, feed it through pipes and then filter it in a contraption housed in the wooden building between the concession stand and the bathrooms. The hole was large enough for a child's hand.

At first Becky did not know what happened. Her right shoulder hurt where her arm was yanked. She looked down and saw her hand swallowed up to the wrist in the drain. She put both feet on the bottom of the pool and used all her leverage to try to free herself. Nothing. The drain was doing its job and struggling at that. Something was blocking its mouth. The low humming noise of the pump was now much louder and became more of a revved knocking noise.

Then two more hands were on Becky's arm. It was A.J. He too had put both feet at the bottom of the pool and was pulling. They pulled together. There was pain in both Becky's hand and shoulder but now they were both running out of air. Becky looked in to A.J.'s face and she didn't like what she saw. He was not grinning. His eyes were wide, his face full of terror. He may have screamed or yelled but it came to Becky's ears in a garble. Together they pulled again, harder. Nothing.

Next, A.J. broke to the surface. Becky grabbed his trunks with her left hand almost pulling them off. She didn't want him to leave. She didn't want to be left alone. He wrestled free and hit the surface. Becky watched, her lungs growing tight now. Her head pounded. She watched and saw the legs of the other kids treading water, their heads above the surface, hearing laughter and music and smelling suntan lotion. It was warm up there in the sun.

The sound of a loud splash that sounded more like a thud bobbed in Becky's head. It was Sarah. A. J. must have called for help. Suddenly Sarah, A.J. and others surrounded Becky. All were trying to free her. Becky felt her body becoming very light and was confused to why they were unable to free her. Her arm stopped hurting. She felt lips to hers. Sarah was trying to blow air in her mouth. People were shaking her and there was the sound of gurgled screams.

Becky had lied to her mother; she would surely be caught for that. Ellie and her mom were shopping, maybe for a cool new belt or shirt. Maybe they were eating at the food court laughing now over some fries. Becky was supposed to be home for lunch soon. She had promised her mom. Becky knew that it would be the second lie she told her mom today.

Becky took one more glance at the wall; it was only a few feet away. The game was simple and had been played thousands of times. Nothing was different with the way this game was played. Nothing was different except that Becky didn't make it to the wall with her head above the water. Becky knew this would bring talk among the adults. Maybe this was the last game. She felt peace now. She wished she could tell everyone how much she loved the water. How she would float with her eyes closed, weightlessly like an astronaut. So peaceful. But this time the great mouth held her, held her in place and would not let go. Yet the peace was still there. It could not take that away.

Red Rover

Thirteen-year-old Zach Jacob stared at the dusty pictures hanging from the wall. In fact, the whole room in the small sheriff's office seemed a bit unkempt and grimy. It was mid-afternoon and the sun shone through the windowpanes, lighting up the dust floating through the sunlight. All the pictures were of officers that were killed in the line of duty in Zach's small town. In all, there were only eight. Two had actually died in car accidents back in the day before everyone wore seatbelts. Four were killed back in the days of Prohibition trying to bust guys running illegal liquor. One was shot by the town drunk when answering a disturbing the peace call. And the picture that Zach Jacob was looking at was Deputy Frederick Lowell, who was shot and killed trying to stop a robbery at Master's Liquor Store one rainy night, twenty years ago. The deputy was young, in his twenties, and people say he froze and should have shot his assailant before the assailant shot him. The criminal was never caught but the townsfolk always knew he would return. They said that because they believe they knew who shot Deputy Lowell and the criminal was born in this small town.

And anyone born in this town always came back to die in this town.

The town was small, for certain, but it was no Mayberry like on the *Andy Griffith Show*, although since Zach's dad was the sheriff some people, including some of the deputies, referred to Zach as Oppie. But this town had more than a dozen deputies and more than three cells and you couldn't just take the keys off a hook with a broomstick like you could in Mayberry. Still, this town was just like any of the thousands of small rural communities scattered all over the country. And like those other small towns it had its traditions, its secrets, its triumphs and its tragedies… like the night Deputy Lowell was killed; he had been a friend of Zach's dad when they were both deputies, close friends.

Someone rapped on the window, snapping Zach from his thoughts. Several people working in the office looked up and saw, like Zach, that it was Zach's best friend, Franky. He was waving to Zach to come outside. Zach turned to the clock on the wall and realized that it was later than he thought. He looked for his father in his office through the glass window. Although his dad was on the phone he was looking directly over his desk at his son. Zach smiled and then waved goodbye to his dad. His father returned both the smile and the wave, his head cocked to one side, cradling the phone against his shoulder.

Soon Zach was out the door and on to the sidewalk. "We're still going, right?!" Franky asked with enthusiasm.

Zach shaded his eyes as he looked towards the west where the sun shone bright on this clear early June afternoon. He looked up towards the hill that overlooked the small town, there on that hill where the cemetery *overlooked* the town. The next highest thing around town was the church in the middle of the square.

Ask anybody how old the church or the town was and everyone would simply chuckle and give a reply along the lines of, *Before my time* or even *Forever, as far as I know.*

That was one of the town's secrets.

The cemetery was another. And that was where the boys were headed. Franky was already on his bike and Zach quickly mounted his. Zach's father had berated him for riding on the sidewalks before so both boys hopped their bikes off the curb and on to the main town road, named accordingly, Main Street, which ran north to south.

The pair peddled past shops and businesses with family names that had been passed down and taken over one generation after the next. The boys had to be careful riding because the road was choked full of cars, many with out of state license plates. They passed the main hotel as they turned off of Main Street and headed west. People were unloading their cars. They came from all over the country and they all shared one thing in common. They were all born here.

And everyone born here always came back... always for Red Rover. Red Rover was the festival that was held every thirteen years here. Kids called it Red Rover and some adults called it the Social Circle, especially the drinkers in the town or teens that had been through it once and knew its secrets, but its proper name was The Cycle of Generations and everyone who was over thirteen, male or female, participated. If you were not of The Honorable Chosen or a Select as they were sometimes referred to, then that was it... until thirteen years later. Each person, if not chosen during three consecutive ceremonies, spanning thirty-nine years, never participated in the ceremony again.

Each ceremony had its own number of The Honorable Chosen; it was determined by what was simply called in the town as The Balance or The Order of Things. Only one person knew how many would be chosen during the ceremony and he was truly the grand marshal of the ceremony. He wasn't the mayor, though, or the sheriff... he was always the town's caretaker.

This was one of the town's oldest traditions. And for both Zach and Franky who had each just turned thirteen in the last couple months it was still one of the town's secrets. But both boys were Just Befores, meaning that they were born just before the last Red Rover and that they would be participating in it at the youngest age of thirteen. Just Afters were those born right after a Red Rover ceremony and were only twelve. They would not have to participate until they were twenty-five.

In the town, more respect was given to the Just Befores than the Just Afters. After all, a twenty-five year old man with a college education could be humbled in the knowledge that a thirteen year old had experienced something that he hadn't. To the townsfolk, it was like comparing a twenty-five year old virgin to a sexually experienced teen.

Sweat broke on the boys' brows as they peddled hard up the winding road that led to the cemetery. Zach looked over at Franky who was sweating profusely. The two boys rode side by side and Zach could see the sweat building on Franky's long eyelashes. Zach almost laughed but he knew it was a sore spot for his friend. Poor Franky was born with his mother's big blue eyes and naturally long and curled eyelashes. The kids at school teased him; girls would ask for mascara and the boys would often times call him Bambi. The teasing had caused Franky several fights on the playground and just as many trips to the principal's office.

Zach turned from his friend before Franky caught him looking at him and placed his attention back to the cemetery.

In a few days, less than one hundred hours they would know the secret. For as long as the ceremony had been practiced no one ever spoke about what happened. If they did, the person that spoke and the one that listened always died of seemingly natural causes or an accident and always soon after the information was shared... to prevent an "epidemic". Somehow the caretaker could identify the cause of death during the autopsy. Death certificates simply read, *Cause of Death: Squealin'*.

The road curved and the boys stopped their bikes at the curb. A walkway led from the curb up into the cemetery. They walked the cement path up into where the markers and the gravestones protruded from the earth. Each with names and dates etched upon them. Some with emotional sayings, some with a hymn or prayer and some with simply names and dates.

As they walked through the grave markers, Franky made an observation about his friend. "You look like you're looking for something... or someone. I thought the point of this was to just see..." He paused, unsure in his own mind *why* they were there. What forces had drawn them up this hill only a few days before the big festival. He continued, "I thought we were up here to just, you know, see who is up here and see if there were any..."

"Clues?" chimed Zach. "Clues as to what we might be in for?"

Franky dropped his head in thought. Unknowingly, he bit at his shirt until he was almost gnawing at it. It was one of Franky's quirks that Zach had noticed over the years. Franky released his shirt from his mouth. "Maybe I was thinking as the date grew closer, this place would start to change in some way." Franky then turned to his longtime friend. "Are you afraid, Zach?"

Zach pondered a moment as his friend had reflected only a moment before. "No, I guess I'm not exactly afraid but... jittery I guess. You know the feeling you get right before a baseball game and you're the starting pitcher?" Both boys played on the same team and each was on the team's pitching rotation. "I guess it's that kinda feeling. I'm excited but nervous that I'm gonna do something wrong or something bad is gonna happen like a line drive right from the bat into the forehead. That's how I feel."

The boys kept walking through the cemetery reading the names on the stones, but both their minds were elsewhere. The setting sun was ablaze in the western sky, straight in the boys' faces. That orange ball of fire was like a sleeping eye, half covered in the horizon. Soon darkness would fall and another day end and those that didn't leave this earth today with that setting sun would arise to it tomorrow. But The Cycle of Generations was only a few sunsets away and those that walked today in this small town may not walk after that festival.

Some knew what happened to those resting in this cemetery after the festival. But others, like these two boys, would soon find out.

The boys kept walking through the graveyard. "This is your dad's last time, right?" Franky asked.

"Yup."

"He say anything about it?"

Zach stopped in his track and gave Franky a hard look, an angry look. "My Dad ain't no squealer."

"That's not what I meant," replied Franky, his eyes blinking fast. This was another one of his quirks when he was nervous, which brought more attention to his doe-like eyelashes.

Zach turned away before he broke down in laughter. When he did turn his head downward a chill ran up and down his spine until his body shivered. What's that saying, he thought. Ah, yes, as if someone had walked over his grave. Which was exactly what Zach Jacob was doing.

He was standing on the grave of one Frederick Lowell. Deputy Lowell to be exact. The date of death on the marker matched the date on the picture in the Sheriff's office. "What is it, Zach?" Franky asked.

"Nothing. Nothing at all," replied Zach. "It's just that this guy used to be a deputy that knew my dad that's all."

"Oh." Franky seemed unimpressed. Instead he got Zach's attention away from Deputy Lowell's resting place and pointed down off the hill, down where a small square patch of land was crudely cut from the surrounding pine forest. There were grave markers down on that plot too but it was separated from the overall cemetery. "There's Runner's Rest right there," said Franky.

Zach nodded. Down there rested the ones that were scared, that didn't return for the festival when it was their turn. They thought they could escape it, escape this town and its traditions that were born into everyone's blood. There in Runner's Rest were the ones that didn't come back but died in places like New York or Los Angeles from heart attacks or car wrecks. Heck, there was even a story about a business man that died in a car wreck one week after the festival, passing through the county. His kin recognized him though and he was buried there, down in Runner's Rest. Zach always had his doubts about that legend though. To him it made no sense to drive through only a week after. I mean, Zach reasoned, if you're not going to come back for The Cycle of Generations when you're suppose to, why come back at all?

At any rate the glow of the summer sky was a rich, fiery orange. With little daylight left, the boys decided to ride home. The next two days would be like waiting for some weird Christmas for both boys.

For the next few days Zach and Franky watched as more people from out of town appeared and the town itself began to get ready. Although there was enormous activity for such a small town, little fanfare was seen in the town like you might expect during Christmas. Too much concern was given to the fact that people passing through might be drawn to stick around and see what all the fuss was about – to find themselves in a small American town where the people were performing a small town tradition that Norman Rockwell might illustrate.

Still, things were happening. People were welcoming home folk and in almost every kitchen, everyone that believed he or she had the best recipe of a dish were busy cooking, getting ready for the town's biggest celebration.

On the eve of The Cycle of Generations, Zach found sleep difficult. He wondered what would happen, had a suspicion but was still unsure. At close to midnight Zach's father entered his room to say goodnight. He must have sensed that his son would have a restless sleep. Indeed, Zach sat upright in his bad when his father entered the room. Zach watched as his dad moved his shadowy figure and sat at the edge of the bed, the wooden frame creaking as he sat. "Are you nervous, son?" He asked.

Zach didn't want to seem like a chicken but replied sheepishly, "Yes."

Zach's father took Zach's hand into his and squeezed tight. "This is my last ceremony," he said. The grip of his hand squeezing tighter. "You stand next to me and hold on just as tight as I'm holding on now... and that is all the advice I can give you."

Zach's father began to lift himself from the bed. "Dad," spoke Zach. Then he thought and decided questions were not to be asked now. "Never mind," said Zach. "Goodnight Dad."

"Goodnight son."

It seemed the whole town was up early the day of the celebration. The atmosphere was like a town fair. It was a bright, sunny, summer day. Yes, the atmosphere was like that of a carnival. Still, everyone kept their eyes on the movement of the sun in the sky as it sauntered across the blue heavens. As twilight approached, things changed; people not going up to the cemetery removed any litter and helped people load their cars. Then, in the town square, the mayor stepped to a microphone and announced that the caretaker was ready.

Zach and many others looked up towards that hill and sure enough, a tall sallow figure stood alone within the cemetery. His clothes were dark while his skin was pallid. The lanky man held a large bell in one hand that made his thin body sag to that side like the bending of a Christmas tree limb from the weight of too heavy an ornament. The caretaker was indeed ready.

Zach's father moved towards his son. "It's time, Zach." Franky was nearby as the boys, as always, were inseparable this day.

"You ready, Franky?"

Franky nodded. He was the only one of his family participating this year. He had said his goodbyes to his family only moments before and now stood by his closest friend.

Zach looked up towards his dad. "Can Franky walk with us, Dad?"

Zach's father smiled and looked at each boy. "Sure. And neither of you be afraid you hear? What is to be will be as it is God's will."

Both boys nodded then collectively answered, "Yes, sir."

Up on the hill, the caretaker began ringing the large bell. Soon, the bells of the tall church in the center of the city chimed back in response.

"Let us go," said Zach's dad. "Let us go."

Those involved in this year's Cycle of Generations began their march up towards the cemetery. By foot and with so many people it would just be about dusk when everyone arrived and then it was for those that had participated before to explain what to do to the first time participants. And so it went this year as it had for God knows how long in this small town and there was no press to cover the event, not even the local paper. Everyone had a job and a purpose on this day and they simply did it... or they didn't. The latter brought the worse outcome for an individual.

Once everyone gathered at the cemetery – and there were easily several hundred people by Zach's estimate – the caretaker said, "It is close at hand. That time has come... again that we must do what generations before of us have done. To keep alive this town's tradition and its ways." By now, all that had made the pilgrimage up the hill toward the cemetery began to form in one long line. Zach's father took Zach's hand while Zach gave his other to Franky. The caretaker stood before them still addressing them, yet one thing puzzled Zach, something he was sure to see. There were no coffins anywhere. That was one thing that Zach thought to see, coffins. In his thoughts, he lost the words from the caretaker but it did not matter. All the participants were lining up in a single row. All holding hands in one long human chain. It was near dark but a full moon and bright stars lit the cemetery well enough to see.

The caretaker finished his speech then rang the large bell three times with some discomfort from the bell's weight. Then he walked away, almost becoming invisible in the darkness.

Zach looked around at the standing markers waiting for something to happen. And something did. A gray mist or fog began to rise from the ground. Zach felt numbness in his feet. He looked over at Franky whose eyes were wide and blinking. Zach surmised Franky felt it too. The fog grew nearly waist high. Then movement started before the line. People!

People were slowly rising through the mist. People that could have come from nowhere but the cemetery itself.

Zach's palms were sweating and he squeezed his father's hand tight; he did the same to Franky's, who squeezed back in either fear or amazement.

Then, before Zach's eyes figures appeared across from the line of living people. Figures rising from the strange mist. The caretaker walked through the mist that seemed to crawl up his legs like white ivy as he moved. He sauntered towards the line of the living who let him pass. He tipped his hat like a gentleman.

Zach understood now. His palms, his father's and Franky's were all moist with sweat as a line of deceased townsfolk lined up facing the living. "Keep your hands tight, boys. Try not to sweat." The advice was coming from Zach's dad. But Zach's dad's hands were as clammy as the boys.

Once the two lines formed facing each other from about twenty-five yards some living folk and dead folk conversed with each other. Things like *Good to see ya* could be heard and *You're looking well... for a dead man, Denny*. Even laughter was heard. Zach understood the ritual now, had played the game on the schoolyard. *Red Rover*.

When each line was ready, the living and the dead, the caretaker who was standing behind the living announced in a gravely voice, "This year the deceased shall begin!" And so it started.

From across the swirling, foggy mist, apparitions joined by hands began to chant in unison, "Red rover, red rover send... Zach Jacob right over!" Zach instantly felt sick, like he was going to pass out. He looked towards his father.

"Run as fast as you can and break through their line, son. Go now and know that me and your Ma love ya." He leaned over and kissed his son on the cheek.

Franky patted him on the back. "Run like hell," he whispered.

Zach Jacob let go of the hand of friend and father and ran towards the line of the dead. The mist seemed so thick and made Zach feel as if he was running through shallow water. He could not make out any figures, none at all, and he was not sure what would happen if he did not break the grasp between two dead corpses. How strong could a dead, rotting human be? Then as he was yards from the line he saw a face he recognized. It was the face of Deputy Frederick Lowell. The dead officer was holding the hand of what looked to be a middle-aged woman on his left and a stout young man on his right. Zach glanced down the line for a weaker link in the chain but he was almost there and trying to gain more momentum through the grappling fog. He headed for the linked hands of the deputy and the woman. He hit them square in the hands, not high up on the arm where he could easily be stopped. Yet, with all his effort he felt electricity surge through his body as if hit by lightening. His body felt as if it was being separated cell by cell, yet there was no pain. There was only darkness.

When Zach opened his eyes he had a strange feeling in his mind and his body. Thoughts, dreams and memories of a thousand people seemed to swirl within him and his body did not feel right but he was aware, aware of the feeling. Suddenly, and almost by command from some ominous force he opened his eyes.

At first it seemed he had vertigo, everything was spinning just like things did after he and Franky would get off the spinning barrels at the town fair. But, who was Franky? He meant when he and George, George Jacob his best friend. George Jacob was whom he went to the fair with.

No, when it began raining Fred Lowell had simply falling asleep in his squad car. He had just now waked from a deep sleep. His car was parked on the closest outskirts of town but he could hear an alarm going off – a store's burglar alarm. He hit his dome lights but left the siren off so he could follow the sound of the alarm. He headed into town, fast even in the pouring rain. The alarm was coming from a store only a few blocks in town. He would be there in seconds.

In fact, the robbery was happening at Master's Liquor Store. Now he hit his siren and came to a complete stop. He saw but one man but there was probably more. The one man was near a car, about to enter it when Deputy Lowell jumped out of his car and went for the revolver in his holster. The suspect turned to meet the cop. Lowell had obviously surprised him. They were only ten feet away and Deputy Lowell was looking the man straight in the face. The suspect had long lashes and his eyes were blinking almost uncontrollably.

Yet, Deputy Lowell never saw the gun in the man's hand. He was fixed on those doe-like eyes. Lowell heard the gunshot but that was it. He lay in the wet street with the rain falling on him. His last thought was, *Who is Franky?*

Black Stone

Betsy Underwood still questioned why she let her sister, Grace, talk her into coming to this stupid psychics' convention. Betsy could only come up with two good reasons. First, it was in Vegas and Grace promised to pay for everything - even the airline tickets. Second, Betsy and Grace did need time together again since the car accident.

It had only been five weeks since the car wreck, too soon for Betsy to travel, or do anything. But for Grace, who felt enormous guilt, it was important to her. Besides, Grace had made plans on coming way before the accident. She now simply included Betsy.

They had been in Las Vegas one night and neither woman talked about the accident. Betsy had exonerated Grace of any responsibility when it happened. In fact, Betsy was the one that had felt guilty. After all, it was Betsy that her husband, Oliver, called for a car lift when his broke on the way to work. Betsy was slammed with work and instead called Grace. Grace was more than happy to oblige.

Grace picked-up Oliver and then somewhere, somehow, Betsy did not hear from them for hours - and she was too busy to keep calling - until work was over. There had been an accident; the driver was fine - walked away from it. The passenger, a middle-aged male, known by his friends and family as Oliver Underwood died on the scene from trauma.

Back at the convention, it was mid-morning and there was some seminar on crystals and their powers that Grace wanted to attend. Betsy had sent Grace by herself, saying that she wanted to shop for maybe some beads or angel figurines. They agreed to meet at a certain spot for lunch. However, Betsy didn't go shopping; she simply followed the line of booths until she was at the end of the huge convention hall where an aged man flipped Tarot cards over as if playing some sort of solitaire.

The man paid Betsy no attention even though she stood only a few feet from his table. She glanced around the room.

"Have a seat," the man said. "What can it hurt?" He had a strange accent. Not one that Betsy recognized.

Betsy settled into the folding chair, opposite the man. "Let me zee yo palms, pleez." Betsy stuck her hands out, palms up. The man took her hands and looked over them like a man studying the pages of a book. After some time Betsy finally began to feel silly as the man with the odd accent looked down, making benign statements to her palm. At least I'm not wearing a pyramid hat, she thought. Betsy listened half-heartedly as he spoke of the spirits and the palms. She couldn't help roll her eyes as he completed the reading with a wave of his arms. However, his final words shocked her.

"You are with child," he said.

Betsy looked on, stunned. But the man wasn't finished.

"It is a boy and has dee eyes of his fadda." He paused. The thin lines on his face became deep grooves as he grimaced. "The child will not be with it's mother but with it's fadda..."

"WAIT!" exclaimed Betsy, pulling her hands away and standing up from her chair. She looked around, not wanting to bring attention to herself. "His father, I mean its... its, I mean MY husband... is dead." She was breathing heavy now.

"Yes. This I know," said the man. "And if the child is to be with its mother the one that killed its father must die... by you."

"What!" exclaimed Betsy. "My sister did not kill my husband and I am certainly not gonna kill my sister... Besides I'm not pregnant!" Betsy thought for a moment. She had not had her period since her husband died, but that could be from stress...

When Betsy looked back down on the table, a lone, smooth black stone lay there. A hole had been drilled in it and a leather loop made it into a necklace. "Have your sista wear dis every night and if she do, she will join your husband and the baby will join you... if not, the odda way happen. You understand? You owe me nothing for now - you go!"

Betsy grabbed the necklace with the black stone, put it in her purse and left. In fact, she left the whole convention, but did remember to get her hand stamped. She found the nearest grocery store and bought several pregnancy tests. Then, she headed back to her hotel room.

All three of the tests came back positive.

When Betsy met Grace for lunch, Grace was enthused about the morning's events but wondered why Betsy was late. Betsy said nothing; she simply pulled the necklace from her purse.

"Ohhh, that's pretty," said Grace. "Can I have it?

Betsy said nothing for a long time.

A Pock of Lips

I remember *that* Saturday as if it were today. And if today's ceremony, with all these people, is a celebration for Kurt Walters' new life, then it is, I believe, no coincidence that I am the caretaker of the memory of who he was before this day. And if Kurt's words are an oath today, mine are a confession. Yes, I remember *that* Saturday well...

On that Saturday, my eyes open to what?

Above me the ceiling fan twirls, wobbling as if to struggle free from the brace that holds it. It rocks and trembles as I watch the dusty blades turn and turn and turn, hoping that it doesn't break free and smash on top of me, or worse, the bong that is resting on the piece of shit coffee table next to me. The one with issues of *Playboy* and *Maxim* stuck to it from countless spilt beer.

Far out, I think, I'm still alive. But I realize that I have only a few sweet seconds more of unknowing bliss before my forgotten actions from the night before come back to collect its bill for my fun.

Fortunately, the payment is not as steep as other mornings.

My head pounds from a dull headache; my mouth is dry – cottonmouth. It takes me a moment to realize where I am. I'm crashed on the couch at Kevin's apartment, a shithole that is a perfect dwelling for young twenty year old kids who have one foot still dangling in college and the other stepping slowly into the real world of nine-to-five, casual Fridays, 401ks and careers. But the stomach is holding tough. No need to vomit, yet. I'm certain that the Waffle House or a chicken biscuit will settle the gut.

My head is still foggy, though.

I look over to the recliner where I remember seeing Cy passed-out snoring right before I did the same at around three in the morning. He's gone. Shit, Cy's gone. I think perhaps in his drunken stupor he passed out in one of the back beds, but doubt it. I call out for him - for anyone. Hell, I may be the only one alive. I call out again. This time I get a response, "Shut the fuck up!" The voice comes from one of the bedrooms. The words are muffled and garbled from being poured through a pillow. Next I hear an exaggerated yawn followed by another expletive. It seems this person is feeling as nicked-up as me.

First I sit up and allow my clouded head time to adjust. Then, it's to my feet. Of course I'm still dressed in what I put on yesterday – jeans, tennis shoes, my tattered tee-shirt with the faded writing that reads, *Yo quiero tequila.* I got it in Mexico during Spring Break my sophomore year. It's the one with the drunken Chihuahua on it passed-out at the bar.

I glance up once more at the ceiling fan. It's still whirling wildly in place as if it was stoned off all the smoke from the night before. Its once white blades are gray and brown from spinning dust and smoke, never cleaned, never dusted. I can't look at it for very long; the spinning stirs the cobwebs in my head. I exhale. My stomach kicks around for a moment then expels a belch. Good God. Stale beer, tequila, perhaps Jaeger and God only knows what else. *Yo quiero tequila pero no me gusta Jaegermeister.*

At least my mouth doesn't taste like an ashtray; that might put me over the edge. I'm one of those *I don't smoke unless I'm drunk* kinda smokers. I got loaded last night but I didn't smoke... cigarettes anyway. My clothes may smell like smoke though; I can't tell. Hell the whole bar was full of smoke last night and this apartment is like a smelting factory.

In front of me, on a rickety wooden stand that is as equally as crappy as the coffee table, sits a twenty-seven inch television. It's a pretty decent one that Kevin collected from some fraternity guy that didn't pay his gambling debt. He owed Kevin a dime and the TV was worth about five hundred bucks new. Kevin let the kid slide for the rest of the money for the TV. Later, I heard the same kid bought a new television with his credit card. Apparently, like most college kids, he didn't have the cash to pay but he had the credit to buy.

The television is a Panasonic and its perch now is precarious. I don't even know where the stand came from. It was one of those crappy fake-laminated-wood-screw-together-hunks-of-garbage stands. It leans to its left, the result of abuse usually from drunken wrestling matches or all-out fights from someone taking a bite of someone's Big Mac when they're drunk. Tensions run high sometimes. Some mechanical genius put a dumbbell on its end and leaned it against the stand to keep it from falling over. Real quality craftsmanship.

Beneath the television, there is a shelf on the stand that holds the VCR. 12:00 flashes in blue-green numbers. I don't think anyone has ever set the clock on the thing. I check my watch for the time, which is as worthless as the VCR. The watch died about a month ago and I haven't brought myself to replacing the battery yet – keep forgetting I guess. Why do I wear it? Habit I guess. Plus, it's a decent watch and I know if I take it off it will probably disappear. I sure look like an idiot wearing it though. At least three people last night alone asked me the time and I had to answer that I didn't know. They gave me a look like *Look at that device strapped to your wrist idiot and tell me the time.* When I explain it doesn't work, the look they give is quite complimentary as you can imagine, like they're thinking *Why wear a broken fucking watch?* Sometimes when people ask the time I try to act like it just stopped; I act surprised and even shake it a few times and put it to my ear as if it just broke. But if the person happens to catch a glance at it and it's nine-thirty at night and the hands read one-thirteen, then I really look like a genius. I might as well be wearing one of those sundial wristwatches from the *Flintstones*.

I make a quick glance at the wall behind the TV. There is no clock, but there snaking up the stained white wall from the television is the black coaxial cable, winding its way up and through a ragged hole in the ceiling to the apartment above. Straight into Kurt's –

"Sometimes I feel like I'm tied to the whipping post – tied to the whipping post. Good God I feel like I'm dying!" Someone is singing from one of the bedrooms. I was sure it was Kevin. The same person who only a moment ago was yelling for me to shut-up was waking to his own hangover. Now he was singing. He always sings that song when he wakes-up hurting.

I walk towards the back bedrooms, laughing at his singing. I pass the small kitchen on my left with empty cans, bottles, dishes and cardboard pizza boxes strewn everywhere. As I walk, a dull pain presents itself in my crotch. I've had this before. In fact, when I first experienced it a year or so ago, I thought it was the onset of testicular cancer but when I finally put two-and-two together I realized it was the result of sleeping with my car keys in my front pocket.

Kevin meets me at the doorway of his bedroom looking real rough. He really tied one on last night.

Yesterday, we all met here at his place in the late afternoon and began drinking beer. Kevin's roommate, Chief, brought home some Jim Beam and we did some shots. Chief was Indian but not the native-American kind; the kind that wears Nehru jackets; although of course he's never wore one. He went by Adam but that wasn't his given name. His given name was unpronounceable and we hardly call anyone by their real names, so we call him Chief. Cy was Kevin and Chief's other roommate, if you could call him that. Kevin and Chief have their own rooms while Cy sleeps on the sofa or the floor or wherever. Because of this arrangement, Cy pays the least amount of rent and bills, which is good because Cy spends most of his money on having fun. He's a bartender so he really only uses this place to crash and shower. Chief and Kevin are still enrolled in school – each in their fifth year, while Cy is, as he puts it, *taking a break.* That translates into academic suspension just so you'll know.

Cy works at the bar, The Freshman Fifteen. Yeah, I know ha-ha-ha but the bar has been around awhile in this college town and about twenty years ago there were some alum that bought the place. They were in a garage band together with the name The Freshman Fifteen and when they bought the place they played there a lot – I guess it was their drunken dream. Out of the five original owners only one owns the place now, Walter something – can't remember his last name. He's a real hardass now and he's Cy's boss but that doesn't stop Cy from being able to slip us free drinks – which he did last night.

Kevin leans into the door jam of his room for support. "Yes, Mom, I was drinking gasoline," he says. Kevin's speaking in his Krusty the Klown voice from *The Simpson's* TV show. This is something we all do. We quote lines from television shows, movies or change the lyrics to songs, whatever. Like when the Yankees win another damn playoff game that we are watching and they start with that damn Sinatra song, Cy always changes the words to, *Start spreading the ludes.* Yeah, I know you can't get Quaaludes anymore but it's still funny. But we're always doing stuff like that.

I always imitate Eastwood. He's my favorite actor so you'd think the guys would give me a cool name like Harry or Eastwood or something but no they call me, Rich, as in Rich Little. No not the Tootie Fruitie piano-humper, Little Richard, but Rich Little, the guy that made his living during the seventies imitating a bunch of people, mainly Dick Nixon. Probably before your time – it's before mine even. So they call me Rich and when I get drunk I'm always impersonating people.

"Fuck, Dill, I'm hurting," says Kevin in his normal voice. Oh, as for Dill that's my other nickname, as in Dillweed. Or, sometimes, Will-deed. My first name is Willard so somewhere it evolved to Dillweed or Will-deed. Who the hell knows? "Anyone else here?" Kevin asks.

I glance through the open door that leads into Chief's room. Chief's room is directly opposite of Kevin's. The bed's empty. "No, it looks like you and me. Cy was out like a light but at some point he must have gotten mobile and who knows where the fuck he is now," I say. "Chief," I continue, "went home to Brittany's house but he said he was coming back here today."

"He's not bringing her back here today is he?" Kevin fires back.

"I doubt it. He knows it's Saturday." For us, every Saturday in the fall is a holiday. College football. The television is our muse and the couch is our life raft. It's not a place for ladies. Believe me, we have all tried. It gets too hectic – insane is probably the better word. And to an objective viewer, our actions at best are immature. Throw in the gambling and most decent women –or human for that matter - freak.

It was crazier when Kevin used to book – take bets – but that became a hassle. It was a hassle handling the phones, collecting money, paying money, being too exposed on one side. He gave it up just about the same way he started, by bearding bets. Bearding pretty much means you place a bet for someone but if Kevin didn't like the team someone was betting on, Kevin would keep the bet and hopefully collect and keep the money himself... but if he lost. You get the point.

But every Saturday in football season there is no other place we want to be. None of us. We even have a saying that we kinda took from the movie, *Apocalypse Now*. The line *we* use is, *Never leave the couch*. It's in reference to the scene when Martin Sheen's character and some other guy leave the boat for mangos and get chased by a tiger. They yell, "Never leave the boat!" repeatedly as they haul-ass for the boat. We adopted it for our couch and our Saturdays. And it always just seems like something bad all ways happens to someone who spends his Saturday doing something considered more productive than sitting on the couch watching football. Spending the day with your girlfriend has its reward, certainly, but you always end-up fighting or something. Always. And you always think to yourself, *Never leave the couch. Never leave the couch.*

Above us, the ceiling creaks as we hear footsteps walking in the apartment above us. We look to each other. We know who it is. It's Kurt's. No not Kurt but his old lady – girlfriend, whatever. We simply call her Kurt's. Sometimes we add Kurt's old lady, or Kurt's bitch, or Kurt's master; and pretty soon we know it will be Kurt's fiancée followed by Kurt's wife. We also know it wasn't Kurt walking around because for one, we've learned to tell who's walking by how loud the ceiling creaks and two, when Kevin and Kurt kinda got into it last night, Kurt said he wasn't going to be around today. Not being around *today* only fueled their argument.

Kurt used to be the roommate here before Chief. Chief and Kurt are a lot alike. Out of the crowd of us that hangout on a regular basis Chief and Kurt have their shit together more than the rest of us. Me, Kurt, Kevin and Cy were all pretty good friends. We all just kinda met freshman year. Well, except for Kevin and Kurt, they went to high school together in a town not far from here. In fact, all of us pretty much grew up somewhere close to this small college town, everyone except Chief. Chief came from New Jersey but his aunt and uncle lives here so he was sent here, for God only knows what reason.

Chief was wound tight. He was certainly wound a little too tight for college and he always stressed over tests, sleep, paying bills, cleanliness, stuff like that. He was the type that could be cool one moment, hitting a bong toke and drinking beer, then the next minute he's freaking because someone used all the dishwashing detergent. Again, stuff like that. But out of all of us, he has kept a pretty steady girlfriend. And out of all of us, besides Kurt, he has his shit together. Chief knows the real world is out there and that you can try to play Peter Pan for a while but pretty soon you're just a fat, broke guy in an elf suit crashing on people's couches reminiscing about some party when you singed your balls lighting a fart. No, Chief knew the score. You balanced work with fun, friends with colleagues. He had no delusions of grandeur and he kept the apartment pretty much in decent order and the electricity bill paid. Kevin may have been one of the first occupants of the place but it was sure as shit Chief's apartment.

Kevin, as I said is an original occupant of the apartment. In fact, it still has his and Kurt's name on the lease. Kevin and Kurt have been friends back since high school and decided to go to college together. They are similar in a lot of ways but different in a lot, too. I think in high school both were pretty much middle of the road kids, both grade-wise and by popularity. Kevin must have been a bit more extroverted than Kurt and when Kevin got away from mommy and daddy in college, he cut loose. I mean he really cut loose. Kurt did the same, but there was something about him. Yeah, he was a little more introverted when he got here – a bit shyer. Kevin always hit on the ladies. Always. And he did pretty well for himself, even if he had to go hoggin'. Kurt was more like a gentleman. I mean here you are at some drunkfest and Kurt is really trying to get to know some chick! Kevin had said before that Kurt had gone steady with a girl named Ellie in high school. He and Ellie dated since ninth grade all the way through their senior year. But when high school ended and that wonderful summer afterward began, Ellie gave Kurt the talk about going away to different states and colleges and how they would still see each other and that if their love was that strong it would only grow stronger through absence but they needed that time apart to maybe see other people and experience new things. It was the basic *New experiences means sex with other people* speech and it really put the zap on Kurt's brain.

Luckily Kurt had Kevin, but when it came to chicks, Kevin can't reel the fish in for the boy if you no what I mean. Ellie simply broke Kurt's heart. I mean, Kurt was so in love with Ellie that it messed him up totally when it came to women - that was until somewhere he found the balls to talk to Faith Underwood, the soon to be Kurt's downfall.

"Never leave the couch!" comes the cry. Kevin and I look towards the front door. We actually have to take a few steps backwards in the hallway to get a better view in the living room and to see who it is. It's Cy with an armload of stuff. He's got two twelve packs under his left arm as he opened the door with his right. He immediately sets down the case haphazardly causing the bottles clink and rattle a little bit uncomfortably. "Fuck!" he shouts, then turns back into the apartment hallway and retrieves two more twelve packs. All four are the same: Coors Light. He makes it back into the apartment before the door swings shut on him.

Clinched in his teeth is a bag from McDonalds and it smells beyond wonderful. He sets down the two twelve's of beer and digs into his pocket with his right hand. At the same time he takes the bag of food from his mouth with this left hand. "Never! Never leave the fucking couch, man!" And with those words he holds up a yellow, creased, traffic ticket.

"What the fuck happened?" I ask as he tosses the bag of food to Kevin.

"There's a couple McMuffins and chicken biscuits in there; I got there just before lunch," is Cy's reply.

"What the fuck happened?" I ask again, trying not to laugh.

"I woke up and decided I needed to go back to the bar. One of the coolers was acting up and I wanted to check on it. Plus, I stashed some beer for today and I left my gambling sheet and picks I was working on last night there so I went to pick the shit up, ya know." Cy pauses, digs a Camel Light out its box lights it then continues. "Then I figure I'll grab some grub for everyone – you can thank me later – I get there before breakfast closes and I get an assortment of shit and leave and head back here. And you know the four-way stop up here that you have to turn right when you pull in to the complex? Well I guess I didn't make a complete stop and this cop writes me up a ticket for running the Stop sign. Fuckin' bullshit! Never leave the couch!"

Cy looks at the TV. "You guy's aren't watching Gameday? They're in Tallahassee for the big Miami FSU game." Cy grabs the remote that is lying on the floor like so much other junk in the apartment. I even notice my high school baseball cap among the filth lining the stained carpet.

While Kevin digs into an Egg McMuffin he tosses me the bag and I take the chicken biscuit. I take it thankfully but before I can even take my first bite I hear the unmistakable sound of a beer bottle top being twist off.

"What time is it?" asks Kevin.

"After eleven-thirty" Cy replies. "C'mon guys! We gotta get our action down! The noon games are about to go off!" In his back pocket, Cy pulls out a folded booklet. It's basically a pamphlet with the title *Nevada Rotation Schedule* written on it. It lists the games and kickoff times for every football game. It also has pictures on the cover of handicappers that appear throughout the guide promising you the lock of the century for only a fifty-dollar call. "While the cop was writing me my ticket, I called the number to get the lines."

I keep listening to Cy's story as I make my way to the bathroom for my morning whiz. I wanna stake my claim on the good part of the couch before the games start and I know this is the perfect time to do it while Cy is spinning his yarn and talking about his big plays for the day.

Most bookies, ours included, have two phone numbers. There is one phone number you call where a recorded message reads you the lines and time changes of all football games. The second number is the number you call to place your wager. There is, in fact, a third number; it is your player number so when you call to place a bet you don't say, *Hi, this is Dumb Idiot and I would like to place one hundred American dollars that the Florida State Seminoles won't lose to the Miami Hurricanes by more than the three points you have listed as the spread.* Instead, you are given a number, ours is 331. So when we place a bet we say, *Hey this is 331 and we want a dollar on Florida State plus three.* That is basically how it goes. That means we bet one hundred dollars that Florida State will not lose by more than three points. We all use the same account and when we win $1000, we collect... on Thursdays. When we lose $1000, we pay... on Tuesdays. So there that is in a nutshell. There's more to it, of course, but that really doesn't pertain to Kurt or me right now. Oh, sure, there is also the Internet to place wagers but it takes credit cards and ours are either all maxed-out or the statements go through the parents, either way doesn't work – and again it has little pertinence here.

Back from the bathroom, I make a move to the couch and take my place on the far end of the couch with the best view of the TV.

"Man, I tell you this TV sucks!" complains Cy. And he's right. Although, it's not so much the television that sucks it's how we have our cable rigged. You see, you remember that black coaxial cable I mentioned earlier? Well, as I said before it runs from the back of our television set and up the wall through the hole in the ceiling where we have it spliced into Kurt's cable. It was one of the things that Kurt wanted to do since he kind of left Kevin hanging when he moved out and moved in with his bitch, Faith. Plus, it's one of those 'cheat boxes' that gives you every channel. I mean, we get all the pay-per-view fights for free; we get HBO and Cinemax for free; we even get the porn channels free! Even when Chief moved-in within a few days after Kurt's departure, Kurt insisted on the cable stuff (he even bought the splitter and hooked it up) and paying for some of the bills, much to the chagrin of his bitch.

One drag we have with the TV is that the reception sucks because of the splitter we used, which is actually located in Kurt's apartment. Kevin has taken to slapping the TV to try to make it work. But of course the problem is with the connection on the splitter. It has to be loose.

As I recall, Kevin, Cy and I argue some more over our plays or bets that morning. At that time we were currently down five hundred dollars to the bookie, five more and we were paying on Tuesday. Kevin, I think, was down the most – something like two-fifty. Cy was down a buck. Chief, who wasn't there, was also down like two hundred. I was the only one up by fifty dollars; I was the only one that had the guts to go against the Packers on Monday night. I told them that you always bet against Green Bay in a dome.

"Never leave the couch!" came the cry. Followed by "That no good fucking bitch!" It was Chief making a boisterous entrance to the apartment. He's from Indian descent, for sure, that's why we call him Chief but he doesn't speak with an Indian accent. In fact, he speaks with a Jersey accent since that's where he's originally from.

I think to myself, *Never leave the couch. Fucking-a-right. Not unless you're going all the way. Kurt left the couch. He left the whole fucking program... I wonder what he saw.*

Chief is starting in on his story about why Brittany – his girlfriend, not the singer – is a bitch. Beers are now being opened one after another. Cy passes one my way and I take it. As I lift the bottle to my lips I realize I barely ate the chicken biscuit from the McDonald's bag. I also realize that it was the lips that I liked about her that night at the party. I liked her smile and her lips. I think it may be her best quality because later Kevin would call them DSLs, so he liked them too. To put it politely, DSL meant that Kevin thought that Faith had the kinda lips – and mouth I suppose – that could perform oral sex very well. Despite all the things I say, or said, true or not, I was attracted to her *that* night awhile back. That was the night that Kurt came out of his shell, though. That was the night early last spring that Kurt Walters, while harassed mercilessly by me and the rest of the guys, leapt into action and approached Faith-

"Hey, Dill, we gotta call these early games in now before kickoff!" It is Cy bitching at me.

I drink full from my beer. "I'll wait for the later games," I reply. "I don't like anything early."

"What?!" Cy refutes. "Who cares what you *like*; it's on TV and you're betting."

"You're only playing four early games, right?" I ask.

"Yeah."

"Give me a half on each." Without hesitation, Cy is calling in all our bets before the noon kickoff.

I miss Chief's conversation with Kevin about why he's in a fight with Brittany. I feign attention until he looks at both me and Kevin and says, "So if Brittany asks, we had to help Cy's brother move in Aden." Aden is one of the bigger towns near here. In fact, it's where Kevin and Kurt grew-up. It's about a forty-five minute drive from here.

After Chief schools us on his alibi he turns to the television. At the same time, someone hands him an opened beer. He takes a full swig, still looking at the television. "What the fuck is up with the picture?" As I look, it does seem that the picture is worse than it's ever been. It looks like we don't even have cable but rabbit ear antennas - minus the aluminum foil. The picture is snowy, the sound seems okay, I guess, but the picture really sucks.

"It's the splitter up in Kurt's apartment," I say. My body is responding to the beer. And what seemed to be a tinge of a hangover earlier now is becoming a warm buzz. Even my stomach is accepting the parcel. As Kevin begins to bitch-slap the thing, I continue, "The splitter that we have running down from Kurt's apartment is loose!" I say it loud so Kevin doesn't knock the thing off the rickety stand held up by the dumbbell.

We all look towards the ceiling, to where Kurt's apartment is. "It's that bitch," replies Cy. "She's fucking with it. She knows what today is." Still looking towards the ceiling, he raises his fist and shouts, "It's only the best fuckin' day of the week! The day we live for!"

"Well, is Kurt up there?" asks Chief. He had missed the festivities from the bar last night, leaving right before they erupted. I realize immediately where this is going and quickly finish my beer and set it on the floor next to the portion of the couch that I claimed. I grab another, twist the top off and dig in for the story that is about to follow.

Here, I'll make it brief – all the while drinking from my beer mind you. In short, Kevin and Kurt got into it at the bar last night. Kevin was angry over how little time Kurt spent with his friends, especially Saturdays, days like today. Of course, Faith was close at hand and, unwisely, I might add, she made a remark to Kevin about Kurt growing up and that Cy and me should do the same. Chief, as I said, had just left with Brittany so Faith used Chief as another example of a boy becoming a man and throwing it into our faces. It was obvious that Faith had too many of her fruity drinks and was tired of us talking about her. She knew how we felt about her. She knew we thought she was no good for Kurt. But even during her tirade I watched and saw Kurt roll his eyes. He was not happy about the situation and quickly stepped-in between she and Kevin. I had remained quiet. But I did hear every word spoken from Faith. And I *watched* as she said them. Her cheeks were rosy from anger. And that mouth. And those lips.

I finish that beer, discard it and go for another; all while Kevin relays what Chief missed last night. Cy is even listening as well; last night was busy and I guess Cy missed the incident. As I start my third beer, I think back to last night and how I was watching Faith; I think back to the night that Kurt made his move. I remember thinking that was the night I was gonna make my move for Faith. I don't know if it was for a one-night stand or… more. But I remember that I was working up the nerve when outta nowhere Kurt decides that he's gonna make *his* move. Good ole introverted Kurt. We all thought she was out of his league. We were at a party, all mingling around. The five of us had just filled our beers at the keg and Faith was somewhere else, I don't know walking through a crowd, when Kurt announces he's gonna go talk to her. We all laughed and I even remember doing some Eastwood imitation, like "That is the most powerful mouth on campus and it can blow a man's head clean off; so you have to ask yourself, 'Do I feel lucky?' Well, do you punk?'" Apparently, Kurt felt very lucky and they've been a couple ever since. And I always wondered, what if?

Well I suppose, before that night, Faith had some kinda reputation as a fun girl. But you know how a girl's reputation can get in school. If she'll sleep with you, she's a whore; if she won't she's a bitch. And, if I'm gonna be honest here as I race to get to my fourth beer, the problem never was Faith – well, it wasn't *entirely* Faith. I mean, Chief has a steady girlfriend; we *all* wish we had steady girlfriends – well, I do at least. No, the problem as I see it, was and is, Kurt. I mean once he and Faith started dating he just went overboard and stopped spending time with us, his friends. Then, Faith, like a true predator knowing she had Kurt at her mercy, just kept him on a short leash. Tensions grew. We would make plans that included Kurt; plans that Kurt looked forward to and then at the last minute something would come up where Kurt would have to do something with Faith. Through it all, we'd tell Kurt that Faith was using him, controlling him; Kevin would make whipping noises to Kurt, *Wakush! Wakush!* And through it all, Kurt defended Faith. To Kurt, we just didn't understand.

"Well someone has to do something about this picture," complained Kevin.

"And we're almost out of beer," Cy astutely concludes. All eyes turn to me. "How many have you sucked down already?" asks Cy.

I look around the room. If there is a grin among the men's faces, it is a shit-eating one. The guys are milling around. "Well, we all ready need a beer run," complains Cy. He stops there, looks at the static covered television and starts screaming, "Tackle him! Tackle him! Fuck!"

"How many are we laying on the Mountaineers?" asks Kevin.

Cy sighs and says "Five. And now with that interception run back 'Cuse is up by seven, so we're down by twelve." All eyes once again turn to me. "Give me some money and I'll go on a beer run," explains Cy as he looks at me. "Meanwhile, you'll go upstairs and deal with Kurt's and get our fricking reception working."

"Why me?" I ask. I turn to Kevin who has a weird look on his face. He has the look of a man that is reliving some hellish nightmare. Maybe it was the interception. But he does not look well. But before I have time to inquire, Cy is starting in on me.

"Why me," replies Cy in a mocking voice. "You've already had too many to drive. You don't live here. And she hates you the least."

"No!" I protest. "She likes Chief the best, or at least hates him the least."

Chief looks at me and says, "I just got here and I've already dealt with one psycho chick for the day, so you're up." He points at me with his beer, then takes a full swig, finishing it off.

Nobody mentions Kevin, not even me.

I stand up to leave. "Beer money first, Dill," says Cy.

I pull my wallet out and handover a twenty. I'm actually surprised that I have a twenty in my wallet. Then I scrounge around amongst the mess on the floor. "What are you looking for?" asks Chief.

"My cap," I say. I find my baseball cap and fit it on my head.

"You are really worried about how you look when you're seeing Kurt's?" asks Cy, though he does not ask it too inquisitively – too seriously.

"Hey, she's a chick," I say "and I got bad hat head." Everyone laughs and Cy and I leave the apartment together, although he heads down the steps and I head up... up towards Kurt's. To be honest, I don't know what to expect. My head is light from the beer but my legs and joints are sore from sleeping on the couch. My groin, where I slept on my car keys, particularly hurts as I climb my way up the stairs. I don't know what I'm gonna do or say once I get up there. I know I need to tighten the cable that leads down to our TV. Of course the walk is short and in no time I am in front of a red apartment door. The number is right below the peephole.

I sigh then knock then wait. I listen. I can hear a television through the door, followed by footsteps. I look directly into the peephole. I wonder if she'll even open it.

She does.

"Hey, Faith, is Kurt around?" I ask. She is standing right in front of me. Her hair is wet and she holds a towel in her right hand. Her hair, that color I like and just passed her shoulders, is wet. She has an oversized football jersey on that goes way down past her waist, to the top of her thighs. I can see she has tan shorts on but if she wasn't, the jersey could easily conceal that fact. Her legs are still tan even though it is autumn; she's barefoot. She had time to get out of the shower, dry off, and throw on some clothes before she got ready for her day. And that mouth, those lips. There has always been something about that mouth... that drove me nuts.

She looks me up and down then lifts the towel to her head and rubs her hair hard with both hands. At the same time she says, "You know Kurt is not here." She stops drying, leans her head forward then flips her hair back sending a slight spray in my face. I smell strawberries. She looks me straight in the eye with a look of annoyance. "What do you want?" she asks.

I'm standing in front of Kurt's. Nobody around us. No Party. No Kurt. I'm still in the clothes from yesterday and she; she is clean, preparing for her Saturday. It's a Saturday that probably does not include a couch for her and all I want is the safety of the one below this apartment. But I have a job to do – a mission. That is why I was sent here. And I believe that it was no accident that I was chosen.

"The cable is out – ah, well, it's fuzzy. The splitter up here is probably loose," I explain.

"And you are the errand boy *they* sent up to fix it. Oh, and he like tequila." I look down at my tee-shirt, forgetting that I had it on. When I look back up at Faith, she's got a real pissed-off look on her face. "Your friends are real assholes. And this big thing with your Saturdays," she huffs. "Hold on a second." She closes the door in my face.

I wonder if this is. Are we done here? No, after some commotion inside, the door opens again. Nothing has changed with Faith's appearance except she is no longer holding a towel. She swings the apartment door wide and gestures for me to come in.

As the door springs shut, I catch it with my elbow and walk in. The smell of cleanliness is all around. The place is spotless. I don't even notice that I've drifted right past Faith into a living room that has matching furniture with no stains on any of them. There is a coffee table – a nice one; this one has coasters and the table actually matches the two end tables that are on either side of the sofa. Nice lamps and pictures are on the end tables and there is a picture of some kind over the sofa. All this is in front of me or to my right. So, this is how Kurt's been living. This is, of course, my first time in here.

Then, I hear something… faint. I turn to my left, where the TV is and where the splitter I'm suppose to fix is. That faint sound. I look at the television. It's porn! There is porn on the TV in Kurt's apartment. And it's girl-on-girl porn as well. In fact, I recognize the one, shall we say, actress but not the other.

I forget that Faith is behind me. "Do you know where that asshole is?" she asks. I'm confused; there are so many of us she could be talking about.

"Who?" I ask.

She rolls her eyes as she stands there by the door. And in my head, I'm wondering why is there porn on this TV? I notice that Faith is standing with her arms crossed. The remote to the television is in her right hand, slowly tapping the upper part of her left arm. "Where Kurt is?" she says in a voice that sounds like I should know the answer.

I think for a moment. I think back to last night but there's porn on the TV – girl-on-girl porn. In a flash, I look up at the cable box on top of the television. There was the cheat cable box Kurt got from his cousin, the kind that gives you *all* the channels. We used to watch the extreme fighting sports, prizefights, pay-per-view movies all for free. But no, I don't remember where Kurt is today *but* I do realize that Faith had to have been the one who put the porn station on.

"That prick is in Aden seeing his old girlfriend, Ellie," replies Faith. "We had a fight."

"That prick," I say, halfheartedly. Everything is moving too fast for me now. My mission. The splitter. Yes, the splitter! "We're getting a bad, a bad um picture downstairs and I think the splitter is loose."

"Oh," replies Faith, "that's right today is Saturday when all you assholes lay around all day and watch football. What is that saying you guy's have?"

In an instant I say, "Never leave the couch." And I'm thinking, *Fuckin-a-right. Never leave the couch... not unless you're going all the way.*

Faith looks me up and down and even starts walking towards me! Oh, shit. "You're off the couch," she says. Oh, Lord and how I wish I weren't. Oh, how I wish I were back downstairs. I can even hear the guy's downstairs. Someone must have fumbled, or scored – bad choice of words, I think – and I can also hear the moaning from the television, the one I'm backing up towards. She turns towards her sofa.

"Why don't you try this one out?" My God! What have I stumbled into? A *Penthouse* letter?

"I just need to fix the splitter," I say evenly. She's still walking closer.

"Out of all those jerks," she says, "and all the mean things you say, why have I caught you checking me out?" I just stand there. At first, I try to think of what she's talking about but somewhere down inside I know. Worse, she knows. She must've seen me looking at her ass or something but I can't be held liable, I was drunk... probably. She continues, "Oh, we'll be driving away from a party like a month ago and I saw your eyes follow the car. I watched you watching us. Last night, at the bar, I turned just in time to see you look away. And, I've even found that you're not such a jerk when your friends aren't around and the few times – which I admit have been few – that it's just you and me you're not so mean. So what is it?" My first thought is that this chick is the Devil. But she's not done. She nods to herself. "A girl that won't sleep with you is a bitch and one that does is a whore; is that it?" Somehow, she is now right in front of me. Believe me, when the Devil is near, you don't smell brimstone; you smell strawberries.

Like a punch-drunk boxer, I try to regain some composure. "You guys are just in a fight," I say.

"So I'm Kurt's whore and the world's bitch," she says. "I know that whore in Aden that Kurt is fucking right now is also his whore." There is no more talking now. She's kissing me and God forgive me I'm kissing her back. At the same time, she is pulling me, leading me back to the couch. She pushes me back down on the sofa. "Never leave the couch," she says.

All too soon my pants are unzipped, off I guess. And she... she has moved the coffee table so she can kneel easier. I do nothing to stop what is happening. I make no protest. The TV is right in front of me; the porn channel is still on but the scene has changed and is no longer girl-on-girl. It makes little difference, however, since my head pitches back, eyes close, ecstasy. Suddenly, she stops. "Is this a hickey? She asks, perturbed. I look down; there is a bruise on my leg.

No," I reply. "I slept on my keys on the couch last night." I smile. She rolls her eyes but goes about her business with fervor unmatched by any other experience I have had up to the moment. My hand gropes through her hair. She responds with a noise that fills me with both pleasure and, well... pleasure. *But what am I doing?* This is *so* wrong. I was supposed to come up here just to fix the splitter. Oh, dear God, the splitter.

The pleasure!

The guys are gonna wonder why I've been gone so long. I look at my watch. Damn! I keep forgetting it's broken! Oh, God, the pleasure! How long have I been-

Oh, the time has arrived. There is no turning back. A voice in my head shouts, *Do you feel lucky, punk?!* Then it is done. And with a whoosh the world comes rushing back. Where I am, what I just did, leading them all is guilt, guilt like no other. I look down at Faith and she smiles. She has a grin that I've only seen on the faces of poker buddies with a good hand or the bookie when we're handing over money, no not even that devilish. No not with that mouth and those DSLs. My head is reeling. The deed is done. The deed except fixing the splitter!

I hop up from the couch. Faith gives way. Whatever it is she wanted, she got it seems. I zip up my pants as I awkwardly make my way to the television that is spewing forth porn that I am no longer in the mood for.

"In a rush?" Faith asks. I don't reply. I find the splitter behind the set. The coaxial cable is so loose that it almost comes apart from the splitter when I touch it. It had been loosened and I knew by who.

My touching it must have screwed with the picture because I can hear moans from downstairs. I hurry, fitting the cable in the splitter and tightening it. Muffled cheers rise from the apartment below.

I turn to Faith, who is sitting there on the sofa with a smug look on her face. Her arms are crossed as well as her legs, with one leg swinging rhythmically in the air. Did I say she had a smug look on her face? I'm baffled. "Why?" I ask.

She just sits there. "Never leave the couch because when you do, the real world is out there," is all she says, whatever that means. "Your friends are probably wondering what's taking you so long," she adds. Damn! How long have I been here? I look at my watch. Damn! Damn! Damn Damn Damn Damn Damn! There is so much I want to ask.

I head for the door but as I do, I ask her, "We're you planning on me? I mean, me being the one to show up?" She just smiles and says nothing; she puts the coffee table back where it belongs. "Later," she quips. And the next thing I know I'm out the door and in the open-air hallway.

"Hey," comes a voice from down the stairs, "you just getting done?" It's Cy, back from the beer run.

All I can do is give a dry, "Yeah, took longer then expected." Cy and I enter Kevin's as we left it, together. But things are a lot different now; I wonder if I'm flush, if my face is giving anything away. The mood in Kevin's, as usual, is jovial. I look at the television. The picture is as clear as day and fresh beer has arrived. The place is already filling with smoke… of all kinds. It is Kevin that asks the question. "What took you so long, Dill?"

I think about saying that it took Faith awhile to come to the door because she was washing her hair but I was afraid Cy might have seen me go in when he went on his beer run. Time is running fast and I feel rage building inside of me over the situation. Finally I say, "Oh, Faith was bitching about some fight she and Kurt got into." Yes, I think that will work. I go on as I grab a cold one from Cy. "Did you know that Kurt is down at Aden seeing Ellie?" Silence – well at least what could be considered silence for this crowd comes over the room.

"Dude," says Chief, "Kurt went to meet his cousin in Aden."

Cy adds, "Yeah, the same guy that hooked us up with the all-channel cable box is helping Kurt pick out an engagement ring for Faith. He has some contact in the jewelry business or something." I feel nauseous. What the hell had happened? I look towards Kevin, who is staring at me, watching me as I mill around the apartment looking for a place to sit. As I walk, I feel a wetness in my jeans. It is sticky, a mixture of Faith's mouth and my shame. I keep walking out of the living room and down the hall to the restroom to piss.

I feel so guilty that I don't even want to look at myself in the bathroom mirror. Why the hell would she do what she did? I wonder. I don't even consider my part in this… affair. After all, I'm a guy and it was beyond my control. For an instant I think maybe she likes me. Maybe she thinks she made a mistake with Kurt. Maybe she was wishing that it was me that talked to her that night, that it was me instead of Kurt.

Stepping out of the bathroom, and heading back down the hallway, I have a clear view of Kevin in the living room; he isn't watching the television. He's looking straight at me. I wonder for a moment if I wasn't the first one that was sent up, sent up to fix the picture and got more than what was bargained for.

I do know that there has been at least one time when Kevin and I have been in the apartment alone and the reception has been so bad that we left that couch and went to a bar because Kevin wouldn't call or walk those stairs.

No, what happened upstairs was about power. We had given Kurt and Faith a ton of shit. At least one of us fell prey to the same woman that Kurt did. May she forever change Kurt's life like she changed mine.

So yes, *this* Saturday, I can't help but think of *that* Saturday, that day when I left the couch.

To the Kurt I knew.

And, of course, to the whore.

The whore.